BITTER ALMONDS

Laurence Cossé

BITTER ALMONDS

*Translated from the French
by Alison Anderson*

Europa
editions

Europa Editions
214 West 29th Street
New York, N.Y. 10001
www.europaeditions.com
info@europaeditions.com

Copyright © Éditions Gallimard Paris 2011
First Publication 2013 by Europa Editions

Translation by Alison Anderson
Original title: *Les amandes amères*
Translation copyright © 2011 by Europa Editions

Library of Congress Cataloging in Publication Data is available
ISBN 978-1-60945-089-2

Cossé, Laurence
Bitter Almonds

Book design by Emanuele Ragnisco
www.mekkanografici.com

Prepress by Grafica Punto Print – Rome

Printed in the USA

BITTER ALMONDS

1

There's a ring at the door. Édith is at work on the dining room table. I won't get it, she thinks, the hell with it. Who could it be? It's almost dark. But she gets up, and goes to open.

It's Aïcha, the concierge from number 31, all smiles and in the company of an older woman. Édith wasn't expecting this. She often sees Aïcha, in the street, in the shops; she's a neighborhood feature, they call her Radio Aïcha. But she's never seen her in her building. Aïcha, moreover, apologizes, with little movements of her head and hands; she'll be quick. She's ringing at every door in the street.

"Maybe you know my mother?" she says, not waiting for an answer. "She's looking for work."

The woman standing next to her is impassive. She holds herself very straight, her mouth pursed, a black headscarf knotted tightly beneath her chin, her hands crossed over her belly. Impassive and tense, notes Édith, who wonders for a moment whether she speaks French. She was working at a dry cleaner's in Passy, explains Aïcha. Six months ago the cleaner went out of business; no one took over from him, and his two employees were let go.

"My mother has been looking everywhere," says Aïcha, "she hasn't found anything. She'll be penniless soon, they've signed her up for part-time . . . well, never mind the details. She can iron to perfection, and she can sew, so I got an idea. If fifteen or twenty families in the neighborhood take her on for two or three hours a week, she'll be in the clear. She could keep her room."

Gilles is delighted with the idea. For ten years he's been giving a lot of time and a bit of money to SNC, *Solidarités nouvelles face au chômage*, an association that provides assistance to jobless people until they find work again. One of the ways they go about it is to finance short-term contracts with the dues and donations of their members.

"Basically Aïcha's idea is the SNC all over," says Gilles enthusiastically, "real neighborhood solidarity."

So he's all for it. It's true that in this household he's the one who does the bulk of the ironing. Édith is useless at ironing. She can't stand it. Gilles doesn't mind, he's happy enough to do his own shirts, but the boys' jeans, or the tablecloths and pillowcases, that's a real bore.

Done deal, then. Not right away, and not just in this street alone. But the upshot is that within three months Fadila is working twenty to twenty-five hours a week. That's all she wants. "I'm not young," she says. You need time for yourself, after all. She lives in Saint-Augustin but she buys her bread on the avenue de Clichy, the flat bread she likes and which keeps well; she goes to the baths Boulogne, they're very clean, "not like out in the suburbs."

She comes on Tuesdays between four and seven. Or five and seven, if she's been held up, or twenty to four and six if her son's coming over for supper and she has to cook. Or Wednesday if she's been really busy on Tuesday and could only have come for an hour.

It annoys Édith. Gilles doesn't care, he never gets home before eight in the evening. But Édith works at home, already it's hard enough with the children, she needs to know when she will be alone.

"I no see problem," retorts Fadila. What difference does it make whether she comes Tuesday or Wednesday? She has the keys. She knows what she has to do, she can manage her schedule on her own.

Already on the second Tuesday she looked Édith right in the eye and said, "I never been to school." She was wearing her wooden face. Édith took several weeks to understand that obviously this meant she could neither read nor write French, but that she had not learned to read or write Arabic either.

Before long she is bringing letters, often still sealed. Bills, summons, advertisements, she can't tell them apart, any form of mail frightens her. She has to get someone else to read it to her. "I'm stupid," she says. She doesn't know how to sign her name: she just scribbles a little zigzag.

She has no trouble speaking on the telephone, but she never calls. At first, Édith gets annoyed. "It's all right if you change the time, or even the day, but give us a call. Call ahead." Until the day she understood why Fadila wouldn't do anything of the sort. Dialing the number is the problem. Fadila keeps an old notebook in her bag, with telephone numbers marked in different handwriting and colors. "You put notebook telephone number," she asked, the day she informed Édith she had never been to school. She can read numbers—"a little bit": she shrugs one shoulder, she has to be able to read the prices in the shops, after all.

But reading the phone numbers in her notebook, that's another matter altogether. She cannot tell them apart.

The most awkward thing is that she can't really get around other than by bus. From the bus she can see where she is, she can recognize the place so she knows where to get off. She can only take the métro if it's direct, and if someone goes with her several times first to show her which direction to go and which platform to wait on, and how to count the number of stations. "After is okay," she says. So she can go to see her other daughter, Zora, in Aubervilliers, for example. But she is incapable of changing trains. And no, she doesn't like asking strangers for help.

To get to the fifteenth arrondissement where Gilles and Édith live, she takes the number 80 bus from Saint-Augustin. More than once she has arrived late, and in a foul temper. "They having demonstration, I been waiting the bus forty-five minutes." Or the number 80 had to make a detour, so she panicked and got out at Les Invalides and went the rest of the way on foot. She walked for half an hour. Why did she get out at Les Invalides and not somewhere closer? Because she knows Les Invalides, she recognizes the place. From there she can find her way. Monuments are beacons for her. With the streets she gets all mixed up.

Her French is comprehensible but full of mistakes, particularly with the verbs, and she tends to drop auxiliaries altogether ("I no understand," "I no come"); other approximations can be charming (she says "He kiss you" for "She congratulates you"—she frequently confuses he and she), and from time to time she'll come out with a perfectly idiomatic expression, such as "I overdid it" or "I cannot say no to that old lady."

She is not really sure how old she is. On her documents it says she was born in 1945, but she knows for a fact it can't be true. When she moved to France, they asked her for her date of birth, and she said she didn't know. The immigration officer looked at her for a moment then said, "I'll put 1945, is that all right?" Fadila still thinks it's funny. To get younger like that, all at once: it's not an offer you turn down.

If her mother were still alive, she would be able to dig up the year of her birth. She would go about it in the way that was usual in Morocco back in the days before they had registrars who kept records: she would say, "the year the almond trees froze," "the fourth year of the great drought," or "the year of the earthquake."

"Haven't you ever wanted to learn how to read?" Édith asks.

"Yes, one time I starting!" says Fadila. A few years earlier she had signed up for a class, in a parish not far from her home; she's forgotten the name of the church. "I no continue."

The instructor had called her several times, insisting she continue the class. "She say I nearly there." The others in the class had all learned to read. Fadila shrugs.

Had she given up because it was too difficult? She couldn't manage? On the contrary. "The lady she say I am the best to recognize the letters." As she speaks she points with her chin and her hand, as if at a blackboard.

But the class was held in the evening, and it wasn't exactly next door. Fadila found it hard to go back out after dinner.

She rarely smiles. When she comes in she says hello, and looks Édith straight in the eye without smiling. If something is bothering her, she keeps quiet and puts on her stony expression. Édith can hear her banging the ironing board, the chair, the door.

She knows she has to sign a check the minute she gets it. Before stuffing it into her bag she turns it over and on the back carefully traces that sort of Z that passes for her signature.

Sometimes it's frightening, the way she looks at you. You can see an inner violence surfacing, about to explode, every instant filled with a bitterness she keeps in check as best she can when she's in the presence of people who are not close to her.

She is so hard, so much of the time, that you find you have to be on your guard with her, always ready to step back.

As far as her living quarters are concerned, she can't complain. Her seventh-floor room is small, but it's "in good neighborhood," rue de Laborde. "Calm." "There are only rich people." Her floor is well-kept and her neighbors are quiet: "A Cambodian gentleman" who's been there for over twenty years, a "very nice" Tunisian couple, a student whose grandparents live on the sixth floor.

Fadila rents her room for €120 a month from a lady who lives in the building, and she knows that's not expensive. The only problem is that the lady doesn't want to give her a receipt for the rent. She wants to be paid cash. And at the office of social services at the *mairie,* where Fadila, on more than one occasion, has been offered a housing subsidy, they explained that to obtain it she will absolutely have to produce the receipts for her rent.

When she goes out she wears a black headscarf, tied beneath her chin, to hide her hair. Her clothes are long, skirt and coat down to her ankles. But no one notices her, no one thinks, when they see her: there goes a veiled woman.

For work she gets changed. She removes her black headscarf and puts on a white one, which she ties behind her neck instead. She wears a white overall made of very thick cloth; on the front, printed in indelible blue ink, are the words AP-HP Hôpital Cochin. "Are you a nurse?" asks little Paul. She laughs, ruffles his hair: "No, I buying this overall at the flea market in Saint-Ouen."

She has a soft spot for Paul. She's noticed that of the three boys he's the only one who is at all practical. One day the iron wasn't working, the steam wouldn't come out. Neither Fadila nor even Édith had a clue what was wrong. Paul had a look at the iron and in three seconds he'd unblocked the thing.

A few weeks later, the ironing board has gone all wobbly.

Two screws have gone missing. "Where's Paul?" grumbles Fadila. Édith glances at her watch: "He'll be home in a quarter of an hour." Fadila relaxes. Paul will know how to repair the ironing board. "He's smart boy."

Gilles and Édith's bedroom has saffron walls, a dark pink carpet (a lovely pink, intense without being garish), and windows with heavy curtains with a dominant orange note. "Is beautiful colors," Fadila says to Édith. "Congratulations! Is colors like Morocco, very pretty."

2

One Tuesday—it is the beginning of March, Fadila has been coming for four months now—she takes a pile of identical papers, all in a mess, from her handbag. They are her bank statements. Her daughter-in-law, who was a secretary in Morocco before she got married, noticed that on the statements there were a dozen or so withdrawals for the amount of €7.50 over the last three months. Fadila doesn't know what they could be.

Édith calls the Malesherbes branch of the Crédit Bancaire, her branch, and asks what these withdrawals are all about. They are only too happy to help. It's what they charge now for cash withdrawals made from the teller at the bank. The rules have changed. Every withdrawal, no matter the amount, will be charged €7.50. If you want cash without a fee, you have to get it from an ATM with your credit card, or go to the teller with your checkbook and write out a check to yourself for cash.

Fadila has always withdrawn very small sums from the teller at her bank, in accordance with her needs. She doesn't like having money on her person or keeping it at home. No one at the branch told her that she would have to pay for withdrawals from now on, that even for just fifteen or twenty euros she would have to pay €7.50 every time.

Édith writes a letter to the bank to complain. Gilles takes a look at Fadila's bank statements and notices that there have also been regular withdrawals from an ATM. Édith asks Fadila: "Do you still use a card from time to time to withdraw cash?"

"Is with Nasser," explains Fadila.

It's a simple matter. She does indeed have a credit card, but she can't remember her secret code. Her son knows the code by heart. So whenever she goes to visit him in Pantin she withdraws some money from the nearest ATM.

"You really ought to know how to read," blurts Édith. "Would you like me to teach you?"

"Okay," says Fadila, looking her straight in the eye.

On the days which follow, Édith is tormented by doubt. She's afraid she's done something terribly stupid. She has no experience in the matter, or very little.

Ten years ago she taught her eldest boy, Martin, how to read. He was four and a half. He could listen to stories all day long ("Tell me a story . . . " "Keep going . . . ") and he had understood that stories could be found in books. "I want to read," he said, over and over.

Édith went to speak to his teacher at nursery school. "And what if I teach him?" The teacher didn't see anything wrong with the idea. He himself thought that a lot of children could learn to read before starting primary school, before they turned six.

Édith also turned to her friend Jacques, a bachelor, a Sinologist, from whom she frequently sought advice. She had just cut out an article in a weekly magazine where they explained that to teach a child to read all you have to do is make a series of a hundred or so file cards with an elementary word written on each one. Cat, bag, hop. The child plays with the cards, moves them around, you say the words together, repeat them. After a while the child knows how to read.

"That sounds stupid to me," said Jacques. "You'd do a lot better to tell your son that there are twenty-six letters that you can combine in an unlimited number of ways, that's it."

It turned out to be good advice. Among her father's things

Édith had found *The Cat in the Hat*. She took Martin on her lap and started on page one. "You see, that's a *c,* that's an *a,* and that's a *t.* Together they make *cat.* Now you have *h* together with *a* and *t*, so that makes *hat.* Look, *cat, hat.* The cat in the hat."

Martin seemed to think it was very easy. School had already smoothed some of his rough edges. He was in the second month of his last year of kindergarten. He'd been introduced to basic reading and writing the year before. Now, since September, they had learned what numbers, letters, and words were. The children's names were posted in bright colors on the classroom walls. Martin recognized his name. At home he tried to decipher the words on the measuring cup: "Sugar," "Flour," or on the box of laundry powder: "OMO."

He didn't seem to think there was any difference between *The Cat in the Hat* and other children's books, and he couldn't understand why his mother didn't want to read more than a page a day with him. But by the end of November, after three weeks had gone by, at the rate of a quarter of an hour a day, he was reading. He didn't need help anymore to get his fill of stories, he got lost in books.

This was a dream memory for Édith: she remembers giving a gentle nudge at the right time, nothing more, putting the textbook down in front of Martin and showing him the twenty-six letters and a few basic diphthongs, that was all, other than that all you had to do was line the letters up to combine them. As far as teaching went, it seemed no harder than showing someone how to string pearls, how to combine the colors and shapes to make a pretty necklace.

All of which confirmed that you don't teach children a thing, you just give them the means to teach themselves. You turn the pages of an early reader, and the children make their own way through it.

And even years later she could recall the bliss, still vivid, of sharing a secret of happiness with an eager little boy, like the fairy in the tale giving the awestruck child the key to the garden of delights.

Édith suspects that with a woman who is over sixty it will be something else altogether. She has read as much—hasn't everyone?—and that is what annoys her, the way most received ideas do. After all, Fadila knows a lot more than a four-year-old boy does, she speaks French, she has common sense and she's motivated.

With Martin, Édith had relied on *The Cat in the Hat.* She couldn't have taught him to read without some sort of teaching aid. Doing one page at a time: that had been the method, the program, and the entire learning process. She will have to find the appropriate textbook for Fadila. The cat and his hat might be fine for a child, but not for a very capable older woman.

Édith has a young cousin who works with asylum seekers, and Édith remembers she used to give literacy classes in the past. A very pretty redhead with green eyes, an English teacher, who rides around Paris on her bike as a matter of principle, come rain or shine. Édith calls to ask her about teaching material.

Sara remembers that they had used photocopied handouts, in a given order; the method was fairly traditional. She didn't keep them, but she knows of some specialized associations, she still has some names and phone numbers in her address book.

The volunteers Édith manages to get hold of don't know of any miracle methods. One of them suggests making up a method on a case-by-case basis, another suggests she use schoolbooks. A third one recommends she try the big educational bookstore on the rue du Four.

The illustrious bookstore has nothing for helping analphabets. The sales assistant looks like a pontificating doctor, and informs Édith that there is a difference between analphabet and illiterate: "First you have the people who have never learned to read and write—they're analphabets. Then you have the illiterates, who learned but have forgotten. You said this person is from Morocco? Try L'Harmattan bookstore over on the rue des Écoles. They specialize in Africa. As you can tell, from the name."

The two encyclopedias Édith and Gilles have at home do not make any distinction between illiterate and analphabet. Édith decides to try L'Harmattan anyway: do they have any books for teaching an adult how to read? "It's not like she ever learned and then forgot." The saleswoman, who is black, and also very sure of herself, just laughs. "Absolutely. You have your basic illiterate French people, who have forgotten, and then you have immigrants, who are analphabets." She leads Édith over to a shelf where at least forty textbooks are crammed together.

Initially Édith is afraid she'll never be able to choose. She can still see Jacques with his eyes raised heavenward—the phonics method is far superior to the whole language method. But all the textbooks on sale at L'Harmattan are variations on the whole language method, with one exception. And that is the book Édith chooses.

Reading, a First Step toward Insertion: A Reading Method for Adult Beginners. The author is a professor. She herself had analphabet students from abroad and, according to the back cover, as she could not find a textbook she thought was suitable for the situation, she wrote her own.

Édith leafs through it slowly. Three quarters of the book are written in "joined-up handwriting," as the children say. The bulk of the learning process will be based on this type of writing. After that comes printing, then capital letters.

The method is very simple. You begin with the five vowels and the consonant *m*; from page one you can already write *ma, me, mo, mimi, mama.*

From pages two to six you learn how to use the *l* (*le lit, la mule, ali a lu*). From pages seven to ten you add the *t*, from eleven to fifteen the *r*. By then you have several dozen words. Then the first diphthongs, then the silent letters. By page sixteen you can read *la petite mule a mal à la patte*.

Consonants come along one after the other, not in alphabetical order; then there are subtleties like *ph* and *gn;* then words that are more and more complicated, up to *expéditeur, destinataire, numéro d'immatriculation.*

It seems like a good method. At the register, though, Édith is assailed by doubts. She asks the young saleswoman: "Why have nearly all the manuals opted for the whole language method?" The bookseller is cautious. It is a war that has been fought for fifty years. There are champions of both methods. She is conciliatory: "You know, the human brain combines both methods. You can begin with an analytical approach, but as soon as you know the words you recognize them globally. Or, on the contrary, you can familiarize yourself with them by grasping the whole word, but then before long you'll be trying to deconstruct them."

That evening Édith reads the textbook attentively. She mustn't get this wrong. If Fadila fails a second time round, she'll give up altogether.

With Martin it didn't even take a month. Édith knows that it won't go that quickly this time.

She spends several hours on the internet. First of all she discovers that there are still many proponents of the phonics method. On the specialized websites nearly everyone seems to prefer it. Édith thought she was being old-fashioned, but in fact it is the whole language method that seems to be outmoded.

She refreshes her memory. The expression is "cursive handwriting," not "joined-up." Of course. What you write is a grapheme, what you hear is a phoneme. A morpheme is the root shared by several words in the same family. You're not supposed to say illiterate, false beginner is the preferred phrase, or complete beginner. But such reservations no longer apply when you're referring to illiteracy as a phenomenon, or the rate of illiteracy. Established pedagogues are encouraging: you don't have to be a professor to teach someone to read. It is complicated, Édith reads, and it can take a long time, but sometimes it goes very fast, too.

3

That Tuesday, when Fadila comes in, Édith hands her the textbook.

"Good," says Fadila. "We beginning next week."

"Why not today? We can start right away, or in a while, when you've finished."

Fadila turns on her heels without replying. Once she has finished the ironing she comes into the kitchen for a coffee. She sits on a stool, her feet flat on the floor in front of her. Édith is washing the lettuce. "Shall we have a look at the book?" she asks.

"Next week," says Fadila.

The following week, Édith tries again: "Perhaps it would be better to start right away, as soon as you get here. You're often in a hurry when you leave."

"We gonna see," murmurs Fadila, tying her headscarf behind her neck.

Édith begins to wonder if they will ever start. Fadila must be afraid, but she doesn't realize that Édith is as afraid as she is.

After two hours have gone by, when Édith sees her coming back in, she asks again, "Shall we get going?"

"We get going," answers Fadila, with a big smile that Édith is seeing for the first time.

They sit side by side at the table in the dining room. Édith pushes her papers to one side. She's been thinking about this first session for ten days now. She bought a big pad of lined paper. The textbook recommends starting off with letters written at least three times larger than usual. Édith has prepared a sheet inspired by page one in the book, where she has written the name *fadila* in cursive letters—no capitals for the moment—and the five vowels. She has decided it would be good to see that very special word *fadila* as a whole right away: it's obvious what it means, and they can use it as a matrix for the first letters she learns. A concession to the whole language method. Édith was careful to write it in big letters. On the special lined paper, the *a* and the *o* fill an entire space between two lines, the *d* and the *l* take up three, and the *f* takes up six.

On the paper she sets down in front of Fadila she points to the word *fadila,* at the top in the middle of a line, and pronounces it. Then she points to the five vowels ten lines further down. She names them one after the other as she points to them: *a, e, i, o, u.*

"Is like zero," says Fadila, her forefinger on the *o.*

"Exactly. It's written the same way, you're right. But this is an *o.* You find it in the word olive, or orange—and you know the sound, o. These letters, these five here, have a loud sound: *a, o, u.* They're called vowels. There are other letters that you don't hear as well, *f, s,* or *m,* they're called consonants, we'll look at them later.

"Listen carefully: Fa-di-la," says Édith, pointing to the word on the paper. "Can you hear? Fa (she stresses the *a*), di, la (again stressing the *a*)."

"This is the letter *a,*" she says, pointing to the *a.* "Look, in *fadila* you have the letter *a* twice, and if you listen carefully, you can hear it twice, too, Fa-di-la."

She has a red felt-tip at the ready, in addition to the black pen she used to write the five vowels and the name *fadila* on the sheet of paper. She underlines the *a* in Fadila's name, twice, in red. "Here you have the letter *a,* twice: here, and here."

Then she writes in red, below the name and just below each *a,* a new separate *a.*

"Do you remember the name of this letter?"

Silence.

"It's *a.*"

"*A,*" echoes Fadila.

"Your turn to write it."

On a second sheet of paper Édith writes the letter *a* on its own, in big letters. She deconstructs the gesture: "You start with a circle, like for an *o.* Then you draw a line down the side, like this. See?"

She writes *a* several times on a line, slowly.

"Your turn," she says, putting down the felt-tip. "Go ahead."

Fadila picks up the pen with all five fingers of her right hand. She holds it vertically, perpendicular to the white sheet.

"Go ahead," says Édith, encouraging her. "Make an *a.*"

Fadila places the pen on the sheet without supporting herself with the side of her hand or her forearm. She moves the point around for a moment, traces the fragment of a curve, then gives up.

"I'll do it with you," says Édith, taking Fadila's hand in her own.

She is troubled somewhat by this contact of warm skin, by the gesture and her own maternal side. It must seem strange to Fadila, too, she thinks.

Together they draw a perfectly recognizable *a.* And then another. And another.

"You see? You start from the top, make your circle, always in the same direction. Like this. Then the line on the right."

But when it's Fadila's turn, she moves the pen forward, then back again. And puts it down.

She must not know what a circle is, thinks Édith, or a line, or what I mean by on the right.

"We'll stop there for now." It is clear she mustn't insist. "You'll practice at home, all right?"

"All right," says Fadila.

She seems pleased. But is it with the idea of working at home, or because they've stopped?

Édith gives her the main sheet, with *fadila*, the red *a*'s, and the vowels all in a line.

"This is your model," she explains. "Study it carefully. And then write here on the second sheet. To start with, make the *o*, the letter that's like a zero. See, they're circles, it's easy."

As she is speaking, Édith writes three big, identical *o*'s at the beginning of the three lines, at the top of the page. "Write them here, side by side." She shows her how, following the three lines with her finger. "After that you can try the *a*."

In the lower half of the page she writes three *a*'s, at the beginning of three lines also one after the other. "Remember, first the circle, then the line, like this."

She hands the two sheets of paper to Fadila, then a few other blank ones, and the black felt-tip. Fadila takes the sheets and puts them in her bag. She leaves the pen on the table: "I have at home."

"It's a pity to wait a whole week before continuing," says Édith. "When will you be back on this street?"

Fadila works three mornings a week for an old lady at number 16, Monday, Wednesday, Friday. She can stop by Édith's tomorrow, Wednesday, at noon.

"Perfect," says Édith, writing it down in her diary. She sees she will have to delay a lunch engagement.

The sheet that Fadila brings to her the next day at half past twelve is one of the most moving documents Édith has seen in a long time. Fadila did not fill in the lines they had started with *a* and *o,* but wrote on one of the blank sheets. Was it her intention to do a sort of draft? Or did she not understand what

Édith had asked of her? She brought only this sheet. In one corner, at the bottom to the right (or, it could be the upper left), there is a little pile of signs crammed close together, untidy scratchings where it is impossible to recognize either an *a* or an *o,* or any other letter for that matter.

Fadila's school age, clearly, is not four, but two. She doesn't know what a line is, nor how to go from left to right. She cannot distinguish a curve from a straight line. She cannot conceive that letters have to be identical yet separate, with equal spaces in between. Perhaps she has never done any drawing, either.

French children, when they learn how to read at the age of five or six, have three or four years of pre-school instruction behind them where they spend hours with pencils in their hands—drawing, connecting dots, learning directions, making lines and circles and dashes, always the same size, always on a horizontal line, always from left to right and top to bottom.

Fadila is in a hurry, she cannot stay. She has taken off her coat but not her black headscarf. Édith holds her back: "Just a minute. When you write there's a way to hold your pen that makes it easier."

She shows Fadila how to squeeze the pen between her thumb, forefinger and middle finger while placing her hand right on the paper. She has her curl her fingers then slips the pen between them. Fadila is tense, her fingers are stiff. She cannot find the position on her own.

"It will come," says Édith. "Let me quickly make another sheet with the *o* for you."

This time she writes several *o*'s on three lines.

"That one's like zero," says Fadila.

"Exactly. See: do a few of them on the same line, like this. Keep going in this direction, to the right, here and then here and then here. Understand?"

Of course Fadila understands. But she has to go. She takes the paper with her.

"Will you come again on Friday at noon?"

"Inshallah," says Fadila.

On Friday Édith waits for Fadila in vain. She calls her that evening: "Will you come on Monday?"

"Yes," says Fadila, "but if I no coming Monday it no matter, I coming Tuesday."

4

On Monday Fadila fails to show. Édith expected as much; she doesn't call her.

On Tuesday Fadila arrives on time. "I no writing, no time," she says, the moment she takes off her coat. "I going shower, sleeping at my son."

Édith immediately feels an urge to play down the importance of things, that same urge she used to feel when one of her sons, when they were little, would come home with a bad grade, his eyes filled with fear. "Don't worry, it doesn't matter, we'll write together. Sit down."

Fadila doesn't say anything about wanting to postpone the lesson until late afternoon. Édith sees this as a good sign.

She writes a big *o* and says to Fadila, "Your turn." Fadila tries. She struggles. Édith takes her hand and they draw the *o* together.

"Your turn," says Édith again.

Fadila manages a stunted *o*.

"There you are. Go on. Make a few."

Fadila draws a few very uneven *o*'s. Some of them look like an *o*, others don't.

"I can't," she says.

"Yes you can," Édith says encouragingly.

Fadila never draws her *o*'s twice in the same direction. Édith repeats that she has to start at the top then go from left to right, curving the line by moving the pen in a counter-clockwise direction: always the same gesture, always the same direction. Fadila does not seem to see the point in doing something so repetitive.

Édith draws an *o* perfectly wedged between its two lines, and she insists upon the spot where she started. An inch further to the right she marks another spot on the upper line. "Start there. Go ahead." She shows the direction of the circle to be drawn.

Fadila manages fairly well this time.

On a blank sheet Édith prepares a line with a finished *o* at the beginning and then a dozen or so little dots for starting all the other *o*'s. "This is for you to do at home. Now let's look at the *a* again."

She has decided that Fadila must learn to read the letter *a* first before trying to write it. She wonders if reading might not be easier than writing. The experts say that the two must be learned together, that one feeds the other, but to Édith it seems clear that Fadila's eye is more used to reading than her hand is to writing.

She opens the textbook to the first page, shows her a first *a*, then another, then she asks her if she sees any more *a*'s. Fadila finds a few. She also points to letters that are not *a*'s, like an *o*, a *u*, and an *n*. But on the sheet in front of her, where Édith writes *fadila,* she gets it right: she finds the two *a*'s.

"Good," says Édith. "Now, to do the *a*, remember, first you make an *o*, then you add a little line on the right-hand side."

As she speaks she draws an *a* at the beginning of a line halfway down the homework sheet. She thickens the dot where she started the line, just as she had done with the *o*, and on the same line she sets out a dozen little starting points.

"Shall we continue?" she asks. "Do you want to?"

"Go on," says Fadila, cheerfully.

"Let's try a new letter."

Another vowel, the *i:* the *i* in *fadila,* the *i* they see here and there in the textbook. Édith points out the fact that this letter is the only one on the page that has a little dot above it.

"You see them, the *i*'s? Show me a few."

Fadila shows her an *o*, an *e*, it doesn't seem to matter to her. Édith insists on the dot which makes the *i* completely different from all the other letters. But she has to admit that Fadila does not seem to see the dot.

She cannot tell the *i* apart from the other letters. Clearly there is nothing distinctive about a dot above a letter. As for "above," it's as if Fadila hadn't a clue what she meant by it.

And yet she seems to have a perfect grasp of the notions of above and under. Édith searches her memory, trying to figure out what is going on. Fadila knows what *above* means ("Once you've ironed the shirts, put them there on top of the washing machine") and *under* ("The screws must have fallen under the table, I'll have a look"). Why can't Fadila see what a dot above an *i* means?

One morning when they were both working in the dining room and Édith could see Fadila next to her, frowning, her eyes on her paper, she had a sudden hunch what the problem might be. On a sheet of paper placed on a table, which in turn is pushed against a wall, Édith's written word, *above* ("It's the only letter with a dot on top of it"), designates the direction of the wall, whereas *under* would designate the two women. Up and down, on paper, are abstract representations. Fadila knows up and down in real space. She can distinguish perfectly between things that are on the table and those that are under the table. She can also distinguish between what is on the paper (the pen on the paper) and what is underneath (the wooden surface of the table). No doubt if it were on a blackboard she would understand "The dot is on top of the *i*."

From there to distinguishing what is on top of an *i* or below a line on a horizontal piece of paper there is an abyss: the abyss that separates reality from representation, the habitual use of space where one moves around, from a total ignorance of its abstract representation. Fadila may speak several languages, but she does not know how they are represented.

She stops by that Friday, without any advance notice.

"I writing," she said at once.

Fadila takes off her coat, keeps her black headscarf, goes to sit at the dining room table, takes a handful of papers out of her big bag, and finds the sheet with her assignment to copy the *o*'s and the *a*'s. She has drawn a few *o*'s, more or less correctly wedged between the two lines, but not connected to the dots that were supposed to indicate their starting point. She hasn't written a single *a*.

"Very good," says Édith. "You're starting to get it. Shall we do some reading?"

Édith writes *o*'s, *a*'s, and *i*'s on a sheet, all on the same line, alternating, and pointing first to one letter then another she asks Fadila to identify them. Fadila manages once in three or four tries.

After that, the same exercise in the textbook, still on the first page. Édith has drastically curtailed her program (they started two weeks ago already), but she won't let anyone imply that she has curtailed her ambition. On the contrary, she has the impression she has embarked on an extremely ambitious undertaking, which is not at all what she thought she was getting into.

It turns out that reading is indeed less laborious than writing. Édith does not exclude the possibility that it will be easier for her to make Fadila read than to get her to write. It's not that Fadila is more at ease with reading, if anything she is less so, but it goes faster. Failure is fleeting, they can quickly move on to something else.

And after all, what Fadila needs is to read. Writing is not indispensable, whereas reading would change her life.

Édith is troubled by the way Fadila crams her papers

loosely into her tote bag, then pulls them out all in a wad—summons, bills, and writing exercises all jumbled up. Every French schoolchild learns early on how to take care of papers, how to fold them properly, or better still, how to protect them in a sleeve, or a rigid folder, in other words how to be respectful of the written object, even in its loose-leaf form.

Isn't it paradoxical, thinks Édith, to want to keep everything written that comes your way, because you know it might be important, then you go and treat it as if you didn't care at all? So she buys a big notebook and explains to Fadila that from now on they will use one page after the other, so she must take the notebook home with her and bring it back for each lesson. But Fadila leaves the notebook behind. Édith brings it up again the following time. Fadila says she would rather take loose papers with her: she thinks the notebook is too heavy.

Édith has been careful not to mention schoolchildren and their notebooks, so as not to imply that there is anything childish about her work with Fadila. But Fadila has probably come up with the comparison all on her own. Maybe that is what is holding her back.

5

Time to get down the nitty-gritty, the combination of letters. B-a-Ba, the incredible open sesame. One letter + another letter = a phoneme, phonemes make words, there are twenty-six letters, a few dozen phonemes and with these few elements you can make an infinite number of words.

To make words, vowels are not enough. You need to start adding consonants.

On a sheet Édith writes, *a, e, i, o, u.* "Do you recognize these five letters now?"

Fadila nods doubtfully.

"These are the letters that sound loud," continues Édith. "Remember? They're called vowels. In Fa-di-la, what sounds loudest is *a, i, a.* Go on, say it."

"Fed'la," says Fadila, the way it is pronounced in Arabic, the first *a* and the *i* sounding very much like an *e,* with hardly any stress.

"In French, we pronounce it a little bit differently, you know: Fa-di-la," says Édith again, stressing each syllable equally, and pronouncing the *a* and the *i* in the French way.

Of the five vowels in a row on the sheet, she underlines the *a* and the *i* in red.

"Fa," she says, pointing to the *a,* "di—"she points to the *i*— "la"—and back to the *a.*

She writes *fadila* beneath the vowels. She underlines the two *a*'s and the *i* in red.

"But there are other letters in *fadila,* too," she explains, underlining the *f,* the *d,* and the *l* in green.

"These letters, listen, they make another sound, much quieter. Ffff . . . Dddd . . . Dddddi. Llll . . . Lllla . . . Do you hear it? Let's learn this letter, *f.*"

She points to the *f* at the beginning of *fadila* and writes it directly underneath.

"It's the first letter of your name, you see? It's at the beginning of Fadila."

"Looking like 8," says Fadila.

"You're right. You know your numbers. The *f* looks like an 8. Let's write it. It's a big letter. It takes up seven whole lines, here, look. You start on the line in the middle, do a loop at the top and a loop at the bottom, and you get *f.*"

There is no point in asking Fadila to try on her own right from the start. There is no point putting her through such an ordeal. Édith takes Fadila's right hand in hers, wedges the green felt-tip in her fingers, and makes her draw a big *f* that fits nicely within the lines over six spaces.

"It looks nice, don't you think? That's the *f.*"

"*F,*" echoes Fadila.

"You want to try to write it on your own?"

"I do at home."

"All right. Take this sheet and copy it a few times. Let's stop now. But can we read a bit first?"

A, i, o: Fadila seems to have gotten better at recognizing them. But she is tired, or fed up. She gets to her feet.

She doesn't stop by every time she leaves the house of the old lady in number 16. It wouldn't hurt if she did; it would make her work on her reading four times a week. In fact, after a month has gone by, Édith reckons that Fadila comes, on average, once a week in addition to the Tuesday. Twice is better than once, but it's only twice a week, and not on a regular basis.

*

By the fourth week, on a Tuesday, they've reached the point of associating consonants and vowels.

"Do you recognize this big letter?"

"It's an *f*."

"And this one?"

"*A*."

"Very good. Well, if we add the *a* to the *f*, like this, with the *f* first, then the *a*, we get *fa*."

"*Fa*."

"And if we put first the *f*, then the *o*, we get *fo*."

Fadila manages, just about every other time, to identify the *a*, the *o*, *fa, fo*, on her sheet of paper.

But at the following session, Édith holds her hand to write an *f* with her, then attach an *a*, and she asks her: "What does that make?" And Fadila replies, "*Fa*."

Édith takes her by the shoulders: "You've got it! That's how words are made, by attaching the letters," and Fadila smiles.

That day, however, she leaves behind the sheet she should have taken home to work on. It's the first time.

The next time, Fadila has the excuse that she has forgotten her homework to get out of her fifteen minutes of reading.

"Why didn't you go to school? Was there too much work at home?"

Fadila doesn't understand. Édith rephrases her question: "When you were a little girl, did you have work to do at home, or in the fields? Or with the animals?"

"What work?" asks Fadila, as if stung. "Not me!"

In her family they had everything they needed. It was her father who worked, not Fadila. She was an only child. "We have everything, big house, goats, donkey . . ."

Mountains, she says. No, not very high. Fields, olive trees.

"Is not far Essaouira." But there was no school in the village. No one knew how to read or write, except for a shopkeeper— the only shopkeeper, the one who sold seeds and tools, sugar and salt.

"What did you do all day long?"

Fadila didn't think much of Édith's question. She was busy, the way you are busy when you don't work: you're with others, you talk, play, cook, laugh. She spent her time with her mother. "I love my mother. Since she die is all finish with me."

As a child she was as happy as could be.

"Now other people my age all reading," she says, changing her tone. She's seen it on television. There are schools everywhere, now. The king launched a major adult literacy campaign, and it included women. If she had stayed in Morocco she would know how to read.

6

They work on the word *fadila*. *Fa-di-la. D, l. D, i, di .L, a, la.* Together they write, over and over, *a, i, f, d. La, li, fa, di, da, fi.*

A word is a gold mine. The day Fadila knows exactly how to read a word, how to deconstruct it into letters and syllables, how to write the six letters and the entire word, then combine the letters and syllables in other ways, she will know how to read and write. The rest of the learning process will be a breeze.

For the time being, what worries Édith is that she is not at all sure that Fadila has understood how the letters are combined. There are days when it's clear to her, but others, not at all.

Fadila comes in, murmurs hello and sets to work.

She reappears an hour later. She has to leave, she says.

"Shall we do a bit of reading?" says Édith tentatively, pointing to the textbook and the papers that now have their regular place on the sofa in front of the window closest to the table.

"No, today I no doing." Fadila's expression is impenetrable. "I no can sleeping last night. I going outside two times."

"You went out twice last night? To go to the pharmacy?"

That wasn't it, explains Fadila, it was her anxiety. She has such terrible panic attacks that she has to get some fresh air. She cannot stay in her room. She goes out into the courtyard of her building. Sometimes she'll go and wake up a friend who lives nearby, and spend the rest of the night at her place.

"What's wrong?" asks Édith.

It's nothing new, says Fadila. Ever since she came to France, it has been happening on a regular basis. "Is the family." She doesn't give any details.

"Is not easy stay all alone at night in the little room," she adds.

"When you sleep at your children's, do you have panic attacks there, too?"

"Of course not!" She shrugs, as if that were perfectly obvious.

She can copy certain letters, even syllables, with varying degrees of success. But she still cannot write a single letter from memory.

She holds the pen awkwardly, with four fingers and not three. Édith has to push her hand down to remind her to place it on the paper. How does she hold the pen when she is trying to write at home?

At times she makes a gesture of annoyance when she sees what she has written. At least she can see the difference between the model letter and the letter she has copied herself.

When Édith writes there before her, Fadila raises her hand in admiration. "Look at that!"

"But I've been writing for forty years," says Édith, "and you've been writing for five weeks!"

One Tuesday bus number 80 doesn't show up, so Fadila decides not to go to work that day. To make up for it she goes on Wednesday. But Édith is away that morning. On Friday Fadila does not have the time to stop by Édith's. They do not meet that week.

"This one is a *d*. You know it. Do you remember where it is in *fadila?* That's right, there it is. If I add the *i* to it, what does that make? Look, *d* and *i*."

"*Fa*," says Fadila.

Édith decides that maybe the whole language method might not be so bad after all. If Fadila cannot grasp that *d* and *i* make *di*, she'll have to go on showing her *di* until she recognizes it (and *fa*, and *la*). Maybe later she will understand that *di* is made up of *d* and *i*, *fa* of *f* and *a*, and so on.

From time to time Fadila brings in a sheet with letters she has written herself on the days she happens to wake up very early, she says. She's fine with the *i*, now. The *a* less so. The *f* seems totally out of reach. The *o* remains a pleasure.

One Tuesday Édith spends all day at UNESCO. When she gets home there is a message from Fadila on the answering machine: "Like other day is no good. I no coming yesterday, I going to my friend in the night, at midnight I going out my house. I no can do all alone. Excuse me. Even if I coming I no strong enough to work is no good."

Three days later she comes by without having let Edith know. She is feeling better. The friend whose door is open to her at all hours is an elderly Moroccan woman who is retired and has stayed in France. She has a room near the Place de Clichy, half an hour's walk from where Fadila lives. If someone wakes her up in the middle of the night—if Fadila wakes her up in the middle of the night—it's no big deal as far as she's concerned, she can just sleep a little later in the morning.

"Is why I put on the television in my room," says Fadila.

Édith asks her to confirm what she has said: "You watched television with her?"

No. It's in her own room that Fadila watches television at night. She leaves it on, with the sound off, all night long, systematically—and not just on nights when she doesn't feel good. "Other way I no sleeping," she says.

But sometimes it's not enough, despite the luminous screen, the colors, the people moving and faces talking: not only can she not sleep, she has to get out.

Édith has her write (writes with her) *fa,* then *fadi,* then *fadila,* spelling them, nothing more.
"What does this say, here?" she asks her.
"Fadila, course."

But the next time when she shows her the *l* and the *o,* naming them, and then writing *lo,* and she asks, "What does this make?"
"Fa," says Fadila.

Édith must not be going about it in the right way. She cannot figure out how to get the key to work. An old educational saw comes to mind: "To teach Johnny to read, first you have to get to know Johnny."
One aspect of Fadila's behavior that Édith finds completely extraordinary is the way she tidies. The bathroom, which is where she does the ironing, has a tall thin closet with one drawer for the iron, the extension cord, and the distilled water that is used only with the iron; another for clean rags that can be used as damp cloths if necessary; and a third one is for the abrasives and detergents, and so on. But Fadila completely disregards Édith's organization. She piles the iron, the rags, and the water dispenser all together in the same drawer, not necessarily the same one each time, and never in the same manner.
Fadila does not classify objects according to their nature or into distinct categories, she doesn't resort to any sort of order. She crams everything in, her only concern, it would seem, to make them take up as little space as possible. Her tidying principle is not distributive but spatial.
Édith imagines this must be due to a chest-based economy.

The chest was the only piece of furniture in traditional Moroccan interiors. One chest per room, no separate buffet for dishes, or wardrobe for coats; no chest of drawers for shirts, or rack for the shoes.

Can a habit like this eventually form a person's cast of mind? Could it have something to do with a difficulty in learning to read and write, in other words, in learning how to separate and order things according to their nature?

7

One day when Fadila again says that the *f* "is like number 8," Édith seizes her chance: "You know your numbers well. Can you read them?"

"Yes, I read," says Fadila.

Sure enough, on the page in the textbook devoted to the ten digits, Fadila can read them. She reads in order: perhaps she knows them by heart, in that order, but after all, that is where counting begins.

"This is three," she says, holding up three fingers of her left hand, "This is two," holding up two fingers of her right hand. She crosses her hands and continues: "Two and two is four. Four and four is eight. Eight and eight is eighty."

There are six apples in a basket on the table: she counts them, pointing each time with her forefinger, and says, "Seven."

No matter: she has a rough idea of the ten digits and their increasing value. She knows how to count, more or less. She seems to know that sixty is more than twenty-five, and 310 is more than 200.

The numbers she masters best of all are the numbers of her regular buses, the 80 and the 43. She can identify them without hesitation. But write them? No, she can't write them.

Fadila stops by on Friday. She seems pleased about something. Before even taking off her coat she reaches into her bag for a piece of paper: "I writing the telephone number."

They are standing together in the dining room. Édith glances at the paper. "That's fabulous!" she says. She knows Fadila's phone number, 01 40 72 75 59, it's easy to memorize. The numbers on the page are a bit wobbly but they do follow each other along a line, are all roughly the same size, and the number is almost correct. Fadila wrote *01 40 72 759*. There's only one digit missing, a 5. Was it because there are two 5's right next to each other that Fadila only saw one where there should be two?

"This is great," says Édith again.

On Fadila's sheet, below the nine handwritten numbers, Édith copies out all ten digits of the number. She separates them into five pairs of two digits the way it is often done in France, since the numbers are broken up like that to be said, 01, 40, 72 . . .

"I go writing at home," says Fadila, taking her piece of paper.

She comes back with her telephone number, clumsily written but correct. Édith regains hope. Working with numbers seems to be a less discouraging way to continue the learning process than working with letters. Fadila knows them, she should be able to write them without too much trouble.

She's got the zero. Time for the *1*. "Watch carefully." Before Fadila's eyes Édith draws the *1*, two strokes separated by a brief pause, first the slanted line, from left to right, then the vertical one from top to bottom. Fadila copies it without a pause. It looks like a *2*: neither the slanted line nor the vertical one are straight, and the angle is not an angle. There is no obvious difference between the straight line and the curved one, between the angle and the curve.

Time for the *2*. Here as well Édith makes two strokes, first the curve, then the horizontal base. Fadila has trouble copying it. She doesn't seem to understand what a slanted line is, or at any rate is unable to trace it. She makes a little head, then adds a vertical extension on the left: it makes a sort of reversed *9*.

On the homework sheet Édith writes *1* and *2*. "Try to do a little bit every day." She adds the zero: "This one will be child's play for you."

Édith runs into Aïcha in the supermarket with one of her daughters. They look just like two sisters. Édith will tell her so the next time she sees Aïcha on her own: she's not sure the daughter would be flattered by the comparison.

"Have you seen," she says, "they have a new range of generic products that are really good, price-wise."

Aïcha gives her an exquisite smile: "I don't bother with the price," she says, without the slightest vanity; on the contrary, her tone is almost apologetic.

And yet her shopping cart is nearly full. You never see her on her own, either in the street or in her loge. Her children are grown and have moved away, for the most part, but she often has half a dozen grandchildren at her place. She's always cooking dinner for six or eight people, she explains. If there's too much, it doesn't matter, what they don't finish that evening they can eat the next day.

Fadila always takes her homework sheet with her. She only forgot it once. She brings it back maybe one time out of three, no more. When she fails to bring it back it probably means she didn't do the exercise—not enough time, or energy, or faith.

But there is something that intrigues Édith. When Fadila does bring her homework, or a sheet of paper where she has written something of her own free will, she always takes that page away with her when she goes home. She never leaves it behind. Édith would have liked to keep some evidence of her work, to try and analyze both her progress and her mental blocks. But Fadila takes everything with her. Is it so that she won't leave any trace of her awkwardness? Or, on the contrary, do those pages have a special significance for her?

She has shown up early. "Shall we start now?" suggests Édith.

Fadila shakes her head. "First ironing."

Two hours later, just when Édith is struggling with a particularly difficult paragraph, Fadila is the one who comes and sits down next to her and says, "We start?"

On the sheet from last time, she hasn't practiced either the 1 or the 2 or the 0, but she has written her telephone number. She did get her ten digits all in a row, but instead of writing 59 at the end she has written 99. Instead of two 5's she has put two 9's.

"Do you know your number by heart? Can you say it to me?"

"No," says Fadila.

When someone asks for her telephone number she gets out her little notebook, and she knows where to find it, right at the beginning.

Édith has her copy it over. She has trouble with the 4, the 5, the 2, and the 7. The 1 is better, the 9 is fairly good.

Édith can tell that this phone number alone will still take some doing. But just then Fadila asks her to add her own number to the sheet she is going to take home with her.

Édith takes the opportunity to point out that the first four digits of their telephone numbers are identical, 01 40, and to remind her that with the ten basic digits they can write every single telephone number in France, Morocco, or anywhere.

Their relationship has changed dramatically. They've known each other for six months, and they've been roped together on this climb for two months. It is obvious that Fadila no longer sees Édith in the same light. Their relationship has evolved.

It's not as if Fadila seems to be really suffering from the difficulty of the learning process. When she comes to sit down next to Édith to tell her that she is ready to get to work—and this does not happen every time, far from it—she is relaxed. In her entire being. She enjoys what they are doing.

One day she brings a dish of chicken with olives she has prepared. Another time some Moroccan bread. "You heat it up," she says.

Édith reads on the internet that there is a great difference between those who learned to read and write and then forgot everything (illiterates) and those who never learned (analphabets). Analphabets are not ashamed of their ignorance since they are not at fault, since they were never given the opportunity to learn, unlike their illiterate brethren.

Édith has come to quite the opposite conclusion. While Fadila seems overjoyed at the prospect of gaining admission to the world of writing (the world of learning, culture, modernity, developed countries) she is clearly ashamed of having been excluded from the world of letters, as if she had not been worthy of it ("Me I'm stupid.").

Fadila is ironing, the doorbell rings, and Édith goes to the door. It is Aïcha, she would like to speak with her mother. Édith is worried she might have bad news. Not at all: Aïcha just wants to have a little chat with her mother.

They go together into the kitchen. Édith offers them some coffee and they accept, with simplicity. At this time of day both of them are supposed to be working, but clearly they seem to find it perfectly normal to take a break and have a chat. Édith goes back to work and she can hear their lively voices, speaking Arabic.

8

Fadila found a sheet of paper at home which she now shows to Édith. "Is my name."

"Which name?" asks Édith; she does not recognize the word.

"Is Fadila!"

She explains that she wrote it back when she had started taking an evening literacy course. This is all she has kept from that time.

In fact, the word is illegible. The marks may look like letters, but they aren't. It does look like handwriting of a sort, like cuneiform. Édith concludes that it must be block letters, as the children call it, capital letters.

She tells Fadila that there is indeed another type of handwriting besides the one they have been using together from the start. They must have been learning to write in capital letters at the literacy class.

"Was it easier for you?"

"Yes."

There's no harm in trying. Édith writes *FADILA* on a sheet of paper and asks Fadila to copy it out. Fadila picks up the felt-tip, but she hesitates, she can't get started.

Just below that, Édith writes the capital letters that make up the word, spaced well apart, and she shows her their place in her name, with the *A* coming twice. She explains rapidly that these are the same letters as in the other sort of writing, and they are called the same, they're just drawn differently. She already gave up a while ago on trying to distinguish the vowels from the consonants, the red letters from the green.

Guiding her hand to begin with, Édith has Fadila write the letters one after the other, and then she has her do it on her own. It doesn't seem to demand too much effort. She manages quite well with the *F*, the *L*, and the *I*. She can't make a pointed *A*, the tip is rounded. "It doesn't matter," says Édith, "we can still recognize it." The *D* seems to be more difficult. Fadila has a hard time with it.

She comes again the next morning. She has written *FADILA* in this new handwriting, twice, and rather well, with the exception of the *D* which doesn't look like anything.

Édith has her work on the *D*. A vertical line, from top to bottom, and then a curve—she calls it "a belly."

She has her practice the *A*. One slanted line leaning one way, a second one leaning the other way, with a point at the top, then a little bar between the two.

When the time comes to copy the letters, sure enough, Fadila manages quite well, except for the *D*.

"Soon you'll be able to sign your name," says Édith. "That will be a major step."

"Yes, my name, and telephone number, and is all, I think."

"No, no. We'll do more. When you know the names of the métro stations, you'll be able to take it all by yourself."

Fadila doesn't answer. She looks ahead, holding herself very straight: perhaps she is about to smile, or perhaps she won't allow herself to dream.

They spend two more sessions on *FADILA*. They've regained their momentum.

The second time, Fadila shows up with a sheet of paper full of *D*'s. She has copied the letter out a hundred times or more, with the end result that she can write it very well, as Édith points out to her.

She asks her to write *FADILA* from memory.

"All alone?" asks Fadila.

She hesitates, then she writes *ADIH*. "Last letter I forgetting."

"Not bad!" says Édith emphatically, hiding her bewilderment.

Fadila is aware that there's a letter missing at the end, but not at the beginning. She hasn't registered that the *A*, the last letter of her name, is also the second letter, in other words that there are two *A*'s in her name, one in the second position and the other at the end. As for this unexpected *H*, where on earth did that come from? Is it some memory? Or a distortion of the *A*?

Beneath *ADIH*, Édith writes *FADILA* and asks Fadila what is missing at the beginning of the word she has written. Fadila cannot figure it out on her own that it is the F, the first letter.

Since she knows how to copy out her name from a model, Édith suggests a new exercise: she can work at home on writing it once with the model, then once without, to learn it by heart. Édith is the one who says "by heart." Fadila says "in my head."

She doesn't bring back the paper but she has been working hard, she says.

Édith has her write *FADILA* "in her head" (they are creating a shared language). Fadila writes *ADILHA*.

Again the initial *F* is missing. Which means Fadila must not identify it as the letter that carries the sound f. She doesn't set it apart. Does this mean she'd be ill advised to start with the phonics method?

On the other hand, given the fact she has written *ADILHA*, does this mean that the whole language method suits her better? She has the right number of letters, even if the *F* is missing and the *H* shouldn't be there—this mysterious *H*.

Every day on television there are reports about sub-Saharan clandestine emigrants, young black men who volunteer to pass through Morocco in their effort to reach the Canary Islands by sea. They pay smugglers and set sail on leaky tubs, at night, risking their lives. The number of shipwrecks has increased because the network is doing well: there have been more and more attempts. Reporters tell stories of distraught survivors, and candidates for departure await their turn, hidden just behind the shore. Planned itineraries have been reconstructed. Those who stayed behind are interrogated: the families, the mothers in the villages they abandoned.

Fadila has neither compassion nor even indulgence for these people who are prepared to risk everything. "People say is poverty, but is not poverty. In the village there is bread. That guy drown, he do better had stayed in the village. But people they no want just eating, they want big car, big house, all that." When she was a child, she says, no one in her village had a car, or a television, or a telephone. People had food on the table, nothing more, but they didn't think about crossing the sea.

9

Early one afternoon Édith comes home to find Fadila outside her door on the sidewalk, extremely irritated. She was meant to meet her daughter at two o'clock and the door was locked, Aïcha was not at home. Édith suggests they call her on her cell phone, assuming Fadila has a cell phone; she does indeed but—the usual problem—Fadila does not know how to find Aïcha's number in her little notebook.

"Aïcha not keeping her word," she grumbles.

Édith points out that Aïcha is not the only one who doesn't respect the time. They have already discussed it; it is the only cause of friction between them and, after all, if Fadila finds it difficult to put up with people who fail to show up, perhaps she might be prepared to see that other people find it irritating, too.

Édith fully expects Fadila to put her in her place, but she doesn't: "Is true," says Fadila, "is problem with Moroccans, they no keep their word."

She adds that perhaps Aïcha's daughter called her, as she is about to have her baby. But since she is already there, she'll come up and do the ironing, she says to Édith, without asking her whether it's a suitable time or not.

Édith is afraid that Fadila will be too annoyed now to want to work on her reading. Nevertheless, she suggests that they start with that, and Fadila accepts.

They go over the numbers, it's a good day for telephone

numbers: Fadila's, Édith's. Fadila can identify her own number without hesitation.

"How do you recognize it?" asks Édith.

Fadila can't explain. She doesn't point to any given number that she can recognize in particular. "I just knowing, is all."

But she does not know her number so well that she can write it on her own.

Experts are unanimous in affirming that writing is reading. Writing the digits helps to learn them. Fadila is stumbling over the 2 and the 9, which look very similar the way she draws them. Édith repeats that it is vital always to draw the numbers the same way. Fadila looks at her skeptically, as if to say, that really does complicate things unnecessarily.

Fadila arrives late, and Édith is on her way out. They make an appointment for six o'clock, to read for a moment. Édith gets back just in time, in a rush, but in the entrance to the building she runs into Fadila on her way out. Her son's in-laws are in Pantin, they've come to see their daughter, she has to go and say hello to them, she's in a hurry. They'll do their reading "s'm'other time."

"Well, has she had her baby?"

No, says Fadila, but they've kept her granddaughter at the clinic. It's better that way, there won't be any problems. "Clinic is expensive but is better. Me, when my daughter is born I no speaking for one month."

Édith cannot see what that has to do with it. Fadila explains that she screamed so much during the three days it took her to give birth that she lost her voice for an entire month. It was her first birth, she was fifteen years old. No, she didn't have a midwife, only women who'd already had children, but they wouldn't have been able to do anything if there'd been a complication. "They hang this thing, up there, so I holding," she says, raising her arms and squeezing her hands as if around a rope. "After three days I no feeling nothing." She holds out the palms of her hands to Édith.

Édith recalls that Fadila was an only child, and she loved her mother very much.

"Was it your mother who married you off so young?"

"No, is my father!" exclaims Fadila.

She was married at the age of fourteen to a man she did not know, a young fellow, a good-for-nothing. There was something blocking him, she says, pointing to her upper back. When the time came to harvest the wheat or work the fields, her own father had to go and do it.

"You lived near your parents?"

"No, is far, very far."

"Was he kind, your husband?"

She makes a face: "No, he no kind. I running all the time."

Édith asks her to repeat what she has said. She used to run away, every evening. She would hide in the countryside. She would rather spend the night out of doors.

Then they took her back to her husband. And she would run away again.

"Were you happy to have a baby?"

She raises her eyes to the ceiling: "Happy?" It is her turn not to understand. "I no happy, I knowing nothing about babies."

Her mother took the child in. It was Aïcha.

A few months later Fadila ran away for good. She hitch-hiked, she says. She went back to her parents. Her father was furious but her husband behaved decently, he said that if Fadila did not want to live with him anymore, he would not force her.

He let her have the baby because it was a girl. She gives a little laugh. If it had been a boy, of course he would have kept it.

"You're a Berber, aren't you?" asks Édith. She is cross with herself for not having thought of it sooner. And yet she knows very well that the majority of the population in Morocco are Berbers.

Fadila's face lights up.

"You know what is Berber?"

"What do you think! With your children do you speak Arabic or Berber?"

"Arabic. Is they is wanting. But is understanding Berber."

They work on capital letters, *F*, *D*, and *A*. Fadila makes a curved *A* that leans to the right. She bursts out laughing: "Is like banana!" Édith has never seen Fadila laugh so much as at moments like this during the lesson, which to Édith seem so very laborious.

There are days when Fadila is tired, or in a hurry, and so she has not had the time to go over what they studied during the previous lesson. She isn't in the mood to read or write.

Other days it is Édith who isn't at home when Fadila comes by. So there is no lesson.

Then things happen unexpectedly. "A lady she coming my house, I making dinner. After she stay is sleeping. He speaking, speaking. Is making me too tired. Is pissing me off, that woman!"

"So by now the baby must be born, no?"

"Yes, is little girl, Betty."

"They called her Betty?"

"No! Is name Camélia."

Édith thought she had heard Betty, in fact Fadila said pretty.

"Is Christian name, Camélia?" asks Fadila.

Not a Christian name, no, but quite common, now. Édith explains the fashion of naming girls after flowers or fruit.

Camélia rings a bell with Fadila. "You knowing, one princess she dying . . . Camélia is old woman!"

Édith doesn't get it. A princess . . . "Diana?" she asks.

"Yes!"

It dawns on her: Camilla. The old woman.

"No," says Édith, "Camélia is not the same as Camilla. They're two different names."

She repeats the names, accentuating the differences.

"And is little animal, walking like this . . . Is little green . . ." With her fingertips Fadila imitates a little scampering creature.

Once again it takes Édith a few seconds to grasp what she means. "A chameleon! No, that's not the same word, either."

Camélia, Camilla, chameleon: to an ear used to Arabic dialects and the rarity of vowels, it must sound almost identical. Even the name Fadila can be written differently in French: sometimes it's Fadela, sometimes Fedla.

10

S ummer has come, splendid. It is suddenly very hot.

"What lovely weather!" says Édith when she sees Fadila coming in.

"Is horrible," grumbles Fadila, tensely. "I no liking sun."

She vanishes for a moment, then comes back: "Monsieur he not here?"

"No, why?"

"I taking off skirt."

She is in her panties underneath her AP-HP overall, buttoned down to the hem; panties that go down below the knee and which in France are called *corsaire*, or breeches.

"Sun is horrible," she says again.

"But it must be cooler here than in Morocco," says Édith tentatively. "The women there must suffocate in their long robes."

Fadila assures her that they don't, that you suffer less from the heat in Morocco than in Paris, "even with dress is this long and veil, too. I never getting hot there."

"But when you were young, you didn't wear a veil," says Édith who, like everyone, has read that the veil has become more prevalent only recently with Islamic fundamentalism.

"Yes," says Fadila, "like this."

She hides her face with a corner of her white headscarf, leaving only her eyes visible. "But I not getting hot."

"I thought that girls weren't veiled in Morocco back then."

"No, I always wearing veil. Is now is finish. Because of internet and all that. I no like it. People they say everyone do what they wanting. I no agree."

She opens wide all the windows in the apartment. Édith doesn't like the idea, since it is warmer outside than in. She prefers the Provençal method which is to have all the windows resting on the catch and the blinds lowered. "At least in the room where I'm working," she pleads.

"You doing what you want in your house," says Fadila, furious, turning on her heels.

She leaves earlier than usual. Édith doesn't mention reading. It would only give Fadila an opportunity to tell her to get lost, and their lessons along with it.

As she comes out of the kitchen where she went for a drink of water, she stops next to Édith and points to the books open on the table, the little computer, the draft copies, and asks, "What is work you doing?"

Édith explains that she is a translator. She translates from English—novels, to be exact. No sooner has she said the word than she is sorry: Fadila is bound to know the difference between the Koran and all the other books, but probably not between novels and other genres.

While she's at it, she tells her she also works as an interpreter. "That's why there are days when I'm not at home."

The following week when Fadila walks by the table, she says to Édith that books are finished. There are too many of them. Before, it used to be good business, you could earn money with books. Not anymore. "Before is not so many people they writing books, now is many."

It was a lady who told her this. "A lady I working her place."

As she speaks she rolls her sleeves up above her elbows and

for the first time Édith sees the very deep scar she has on the inside of her right arm, at least eight inches long.

She was locked in, she broke a window pane to get out, and cut her forearm, she says, with no further explanation, then abruptly raises her chin.

Édith runs into Aïcha in the street, a festive fiftysomething, a grandmother in jeans. She congratulates her on the birth of her granddaughter. "A girl is better than nothing," concedes Aïcha graciously.

They are standing in line together at the boulangerie. Édith brings up what Fadila told her about her marriage.

"She was fourteen . . ."

"It was rape," says Aïcha, not beating around the bush. "She used to do the laundry at night, did she tell you that? She was so afraid to go to bed with her husband that she began to do the laundry, when really it was time to go to bed. He called to her from the bedroom, shouting all through the house. She would say, I'm coming, but first I have to hang up the washing. She went up on the terrace and was as slow about it as she could be, hoping he'd fall asleep in the meantime."

She shrugs: "I don't know why she goes around saying she doesn't know how old she is. She had me when she was fifteen. I'm fifty, she can just count on her fingers."

Even at the end of the afternoon it is hot. They drink some orange juice in the kitchen then move into the dining room and sit down to work. Édith says, "Can you write your name for me in your head?" and Fadila complies, without any mistakes.

Édith is exultant and claps her hands.

"Is no important," says Fadila.

"What do you mean! You write your name without hesitating, and absolutely correctly: I call that important!"

Three and a half months to get this far: Édith's no fool, it has taken a long time. But at the rate of fifteen minutes a session—twenty minutes now and again—it isn't so long, really.

"And now it's time to start on your last name," she says, writing out *AMRANI* in capital letters.

Fadila knows that, like everyone, she has a first and last name. She knows that she is not the only one with the last name Amrani, and that there are a lot of Fadilas as well, but, she says, "Is only one Fadila Amrani."

Édith deconstructs *Amrani* into three syllables, more out of habit than conviction. With a pencil she draws a circle around each syllable. She says them out loud, *AM, RA, NI* and tries to get Fadila to say them; Fadila isn't in the mood.

She points out that the first syllable is made up of two letters, the *A* that she now knows well, and an *M*. Édith holds Fadila's hand and explains the graphic composition of the letter as she writes it with her: a straight line from top to bottom, then a little slanted line this way, another slanted line the other way, and then yet another big straight line from top to bottom.

Fadila can't get it. "Keep trying," says Édith. "It will come."

Fadila draws two parallel vertical lines and then, between the two of them, the two slanted lines, perfectly correctly.

Édith sits up straight, raising her hands: "That's great! You've got it. You've found your own way of writing it, that's a good way to learn. Go on, do another one."

For their next lesson, Fadila will write more *M*'s and *AM*'s, and copy out *AMRANI*.

This time it is Fadila who asks Édith if she has time for a lesson. But you can't be at your best every day: she can't write her first name from memory anymore, and she hasn't got the *AM* at all; the letter *A* is not as well drawn as the previous time and the *M* doesn't come out right.

From long ago, from her own years of primary school, Édith hears the voice of a cantankerous woman harping on,

"Rome wasn't built in a day." A phrase that she did not find the least bit encouraging.

They work on the *M* and the *A*. Things are looking up.

Édith has an idea, an idea so patently elementary that she cannot help, once again, but take the measure of how modest her aims with Fadila have become. She takes a sheet of fine cardboard and a thick black felt-tip pen from the shelf where she has a small stationery supply. On the white cardboard she writes, in big capital letters, *FADILA AMRANI*.

"Take it home with you. Put it up in a good spot where you can see it. Somewhere in the kitchen, for example."

"No, I putting on television," says Fadila. "Like that, is going into the eyes."

After Fadila has gone home, Édith takes another sheet of cardboard and writes the same two words on it, then looks for a place to put it in the bathroom. She imagines Fadila there ironing, her back to the window, so she pins it to the wall just opposite, at eye level.

The following time, as she is setting up the ironing board, Fadila sees it at once. It makes her laugh. But it bothers her, too:

"What is saying, you husband?"

"He thinks it's a very pretty name," says Édith, and she isn't lying.

They work on *AMRANI*. The *M* is still giving Fadila trouble. She calls it, "that one I no liking."

They have to keep going. "Let's try the *R* now." Édith circles the letter that is in the third position in her name.

"I knowing that one," says Fadila. "Is train, RER A, RER B, RER C."

Excellent. Édith writes *RER*, shows her that the letter *R* comes up twice and, while she's at it, points to the letter *E* in between. Next to it she writes the letter *A*.

"I knowing that one," says Fadila again.

"Of course you do, you know the *A*."

"I knowing the *B*, too."

She explains that *B* is the first letter of the code for the electronic lock outside her building.

Édith would like to seize the opportunity to have her work on the code, but Fadila, who knows how to do it—she mimes the gesture with her index finger—cannot remember what comes after the *B*.

"It's probably numbers, no?"

She can't remember.

Fadila copies out *RER A*, *RER B*, and *RER C*, quickly and neatly. Yet they had never studied the *E*. It's the first time she's written it, and she manages to draw it without any trouble, or so it would seem.

On a sheet of paper, in a column, Édith writes *RER A*, *RER B*, *RER C*, and beneath it, *FADILA AMRANI*. She asks Fadila to find the letters that are shared by all these words. Fadila can't see it. She knows *A* and *B*. She has just copied out *R* and *E*. But to find these same letters within a word must require other skills: she can't do it.

11

I so tired," she says, as soon as she comes in. It's the heat. But there's something else, too. "All morning is arguing with Madame Aubin." This lady lives in her building on rue de Laborde, and Fadila works for her on Tuesday mornings. The woman lives with her twenty-five-year-old daughter and cannot put up with her anymore. She is over-wrought because of it and takes it out on Fadila.

"What does that girl do, then, to annoy her mother so much?"

"Alice?"

Fadila likes the girl. She's watched her grow up. She's a chubby young woman who always wears black. "She thinking with black no one seeing how she is fat!" She has just found a job and is making a good living. "She shopping, shopping, makeup, shoes, bags . . . Her room is so many things, looking like department store." She wears things once and leaves them to be washed, "Madame Aubin she going crazy."

After a pause she says, "I writing very much yesterday."

"Good," says Édith. "Let's go over your name, *AMRANI*. Go ahead, write the beginning, *AM*."

With no model to copy from, Fadila makes a perfect *M*. Édith congratulates her and asks her to put an *A* first: "You know, the first letter of your name."

Fadila makes an *F*. She must have mixed up first and last names. In any event, she's written the first letter of her first name. So now she knows how to single out the first letter of a word, thinks Édith, but if she's honest she knows that's not at all sure.

But the fact that Édith has asked her to write *A*, the first letter of her last name, and Fadila has written *F*, the first letter of her first name, is troubling: it means she doesn't know what the few letters she does know how to write are called.

With the model in front of her Fadila can copy out her first and last names flawlessly.

"Superb," says Édith. "Before you go, can you write *FADILA* for me in your head?"

Fadila writes *FAILA*. Without the model she cannot tell which letter is missing. With the model, and a bit of effort, she can get it.

Édith hands her the sheet where she did such a good job of copying out her first and last name, and says, "Soon, you'll see, you'll know them both by heart."

Édith needs someone to take over from her, a literacy course where she can enroll Fadila. It's just going too slowly; they're not making any headway. Fadila has to be made to work every day.

Above all she needs to have real classes, given by good professionals. Édith hasn't known how to go about it. She's been feeling her way, and hasn't found either a method or the trigger.

And vacation time is coming. At the end of July Fadila will be leaving for Casablanca to stay with a cousin. By the time she gets back, Édith and her family will have left Paris in turn. If she comes to work at their place while they're gone, she'll see no one. Come September, what will she remember of the little she has learned?

Édith goes through the many literacy centers listed in the west of Paris. Fadila agrees to take a course when she gets back on condition that it is in the evening. During the day she is "working." And her schedule is not regular, she explains to

Édith—who had already noticed as much. She can't commit to taking a class before seven or eight in the evening.

Will she have the energy to go back out at night after a full workday? She'd found it hard the first time round. Fadila assures Édith that this time is different. She knows it was a mistake to drop out. She won't do it again, she'll stick with it.

By the looks of it there is only one association that offers evening classes. Édith calls them up. The association has thirty years' experience. It is run by volunteers. The classes are held in the parish hall in Saint-Landry, in the ninth arrondissement. Fadila can even get there on foot.

She has the impression that that's where she began, several years ago, before she gave up, but she doesn't mind. The enrolment session will be held on Wednesday, September 7th, in the evening. During the meeting they'll divide the participants into little groups, depending on their level. Édith and Fadila will see each other again before then, and they'll discuss it again. "Inshallah," says Fadila.

She's promises to practice while she's in Morocco. She'll go over what she's learned, a little bit every day. Édith gives her worksheets to take with her: the ten numbers, her telephone number, *FADILA AMRANI, RER A, RER B, RER C*—it is so little, she sees, when it's written down in black and white like this. She gives herself a shake: two or three keys don't weigh very much, either, yet they're precious.

"Maybe while you're at your cousins' someone could do some writing with you?" suggests Édith.

"I no think so." Fadila frowns.

Perhaps at her age she really doesn't feel like putting herself in the position of the pupil among members of her family, or letting them see how difficult it is for her to make any progress.

12

É dith comes back to Paris at the end of August, shortly before the rest of her family. She has a job accompanying an American novelist whose books she has translated, to act as an interpreter.

Fadila has been there in her absence. There was a mountain of laundry to be ironed. "Let me know how long it took you," Édith had told her.

As soon as she comes in she sees on the dining room table a yellow post-it which Fadila took from her pad next to the telephone: on it she has written *FADILA 4*. The *4* is a bit misshapen, it looks like a *K*, but it is clear enough.

They see each other two days later. Fadila is in a good mood.

"Thank you for your little note," says Édith.

"You understand?" asks Fadila, radiant.

"Absolutely. You wrote down four hours."

"I writing too the old lady her code."

She explains to Édith that at number 16 on her street, where she goes three mornings a week, the electronic code to the entrance has just changed. The old lady called her two days ago to give her the new code. But she was very worried that Fadila would not be able to remember it.

"He say, you going remember? I say, I gonna writing. He say *B 24 09* and I writing."

"Did she say *B* or *P*?" asks Édith, equally concerned.

Fadila pronounces her *P*'s like *B*'s; it seems to Édith that she has heard there is no *p* sound in Arabic.

Fadila picks up one of Édith's felt-tips, and takes a sheet of paper: "I making *B* my way," she warns, writing a perfectly recognizable *B*.

She adds the four digits of the code. These she remembers. And writes in her own way; it's not that easy to tell the *2* from the *9*. But she manages.

"Did it work? Had you written the right code down?"

"Is working!"

She was sick in Morocco. She cannot stand the spices. "In Morocco I always getting sick."

"And besides that? Your vacation?"

"Bah." She raises one shoulder.

"Did things go all right with your cousin?"

The cousin, yes, but not the cousin's husband. Fadila winces. He's Algerian, and she doesn't like Algerians. "Moroccans is no liking Algerians," she says bluntly.

"Do you still have a house in Morocco?"

"Yes! Is big house on the mountain next to Essaouira."

"The house where you grew up?"

"Yes, is my house. But is my brother living there with his wife."

"I thought you were an only child."

Her father and mother had no other children, she explains graciously. But when she found herself alone in Rabat with her three children, she had to earn her living. She left the house at seven in the morning and came home at eight in the evening. Her mother came to keep house and look after the children. "I loving my mother very much; since she die is all finish with me," she says, word for word the same formula Édith has already heard.

The two women were quite pleased with this arrangement,

but someone who was not so pleased was Fadila's father, who had stayed behind on his own in the village. He ordered his wife to come back, to no avail. She didn't want to. So he took a second wife who gave him a son. It is this son whom Fadila calls her brother. He is twenty-five years younger and Fadila has never seen him. She knows he has a wife and children and that he lives in the family home. She supposes he lives the way people have always lived there, from the land.

Fadila's mother was first to die, a long time ago, then her father, whom neither she nor her mother ever saw again, and finally her father's second wife.

For Édith, Fadila's story had left off when she was fifteen, living with her parents in the village, at the moment of Aïcha's birth. She did not know that Fadila had gone on to live and work, on her own with her children, in Rabat.

"You were married twice?"

"Three times." Fadila lifts three fingers of her right hand. "All three husbands is bad husbands," she adds. "Enough, I got to do ironing. You listening, I talking all the time, I has ironing, after all!"

"Don't forget that next Wednesday evening, the 7th, is the day to enroll at the association."

"Yes, of course, I remembering."

"If you like, I can go to the meeting with you."

"Is nice of you. Okay."

Édith would like to find out which type of writing they use with their beginners, and to tell the instructor that Fadila is more at ease with capital letters than with cursive handwriting. She's afraid the class might use cursive.

"It would be good if we did some work beforehand."

"Have to!" says Fadila. "If I enrolling next week . . ."

She goes to fetch her bag from where she left it in the hallway.

"Is no gonna be easy," she continues. But she does not seem to be particularly worried, her tone is the same as when she finishes a sentence referring to the future with "inshallah."

She takes a piece of paper from her shopping bag. On it she has written *FADILA AMRANI* twenty or more times, flawlessly, in a column.

Édith wasn't expecting this. "You've been working hard!"

"Is okay, I know my name," Fadila says forcefully. "Let's doing something else."

This is the first time she has asserted that something has been learned and it is time to move on.

She is sitting at her usual place at the dining room table. She's not in a hurry today. Édith sits down in turn, places a few pieces of paper between them and asks her to write her first name from memory. Fadila does it without making any mistakes, first time round.

"Perfect. Now your last name, Amrani."

Fadila's hand hovers in the air.

"Begin with *AM*," says Édith, "*A*, then *M*."

Fadila writes *M*.

"That's a good *M*, but to write *AM*, remember, you need one other letter, too . . ."

"Yes," says Fadila, "the letter there and there."

Fadila points with her fingertip to the two *A*'s in Fadila. She writes an *A*, not before the *M* but after.

Next to this *MA*, Édith writes *AM*, explains that *MA* is pronounced *ma* and is not the same thing as *AM*, which is pronounced *am*.

She writes *AMRANI* and asks Fadila to copy her name. Fadila writes *MRANI*. "There's a letter missing," Édith says. Fadila cannot see which one is missing.

Enough difficulty for now. Édith says again, "Your name begins with *A*, you know the *A*," and at the same time she adds it to *MRANI*, where it belongs, at the beginning.

Fadila has trouble doing the same. She doesn't know how to reconstruct a word. Édith cannot figure out why.

"In any event"—she is speaking to herself as much as to Fadila—"you've got your first name, you know how to write it now."

She writes first and last name on a sheet of paper and asks Fadila to copy them out at home, first from the model, then on another sheet of paper on her own.

Fadila takes the papers and gets up, telling Édith all the while that the night before, her son called her on the phone, and she knew it was him before she picked up because his name was displayed on the little screen. "Is called Nasser," she says, "But is name is Larbit. I seeing Larbit."

"Like this?" asks Édith, hastily writing *LARBIT*.

"Yes. 'Xactly like that."

"That's great!" says Édith.

This time, she explains, Fadila has read a word that she learned to recognize all on her own. One day soon she will be able to read other words she's learned on her own. And from then on she will know how to read. She's getting there.

Édith calls the Association Saint-Landry to make sure that the enrollment session is still scheduled for the 7th in the evening. One of the organizers has taken her call; he asks her a few questions about Fadila, then sounds exasperated when he finds out how old she is. He warns Édith that there will be a lot of people on the 7th, and they won't be able to take everyone. Given how hard it is for older people to learn to read and write, and how disappointing the results can be, the younger students will have priority.

"Obviously," says the man, "we don't know yet how old the participants will be, and whether your protégée will be one of the oldest or not. No point upsetting her; don't say anything to her about it."

*

Fadila brings back the paper where she was supposed to copy out her first and last name. Underneath *FADILA AMRANI* she has written

FADNI
FADIANI
AMAILA
AMRIL

Four words using the letters from her first and last name, but in fact she was supposed to copy them from the model.

As cheerfully as possible Édith says, "You haven't got everything, there are bits missing. You're doing great on your capital letters now."

She does not dare ask who wrote the flawless column of names Fadila has brought back with her from Morocco. She hides the sheet where first and last name have been scrunched together so dishearteningly, and writes Fadila's name out again on a clean sheet. "Your turn now," she says. "Look at it carefully and copy it out, the whole thing. Don't leave anything out!"

Fadila laughs. She writes *FADIAAMRANI*.

Édith draws a line between the two *A*'s in the middle. Underneath she rewrites the first and last names, carefully separated by a space, and she points to the space. "Words mustn't be stuck together in French, remember? Go on, write the two words again, each one separately."

Fadila writes *FADILA MRANI* with a tiny space between the two.

Édith shows her that there is a letter missing from the beginning of the name. "Oh, right, is missing," says Fadila, and she writes an *A* in the little space she had left between first and last names, effectively joining them together.

The enrollment session at the association is for tomorrow evening at eight P.M.

"Do you want to meet there?" asks Édith.

Fadila suggests, rather, that Édith come by her place at the end of the day, at around seven, and they will go together to the rue Saint-Landry.

13

S tairway B, is other side courtyard," Fadila told her. "You taking elevator all the way to sixth floor. Is first room."

The courtyard is long, expansive, and calm, with three trees planted in a row. The building at the end is solid, and the sixth floor is light and well maintained. But Fadila's room is tiny. Inhuman—the word immediately springs to mind. It must be six feet wide by eight feet long, and the ceiling is no higher than six feet either. It has everything—a bed, sink, fridge, hot plate, microwave, and television, and a few stacking boxes for storage. The passage between the bed and the furniture, leading from the door to the window opposite, is so narrow that two people cannot pass each other. The window may well look out onto the sky, and when you draw closer there is a view of rooftops as far as the eye can see, but it is no wonder that Fadila has panic attacks living in such cramped quarters. It would be abnormal if she didn't. At a push you can sleep in such a confined space, but you cannot stand up in there, you cannot live. In a place like this a television is so much more than mere distraction: it becomes an opening onto the world in the most physical way, a vital source of space and air.

Fadila has made some tea—she has noticed that Édith drinks tea all the time—to go with some almonds and a store-bought pound cake. She hands two slices to Édith straight off and says, "Is very good. I'm eating every morning for breakfast."

She adds, "I having nothing, no money, room is small, I no telling nobody I have big house or money. I telling the truth."

Her honesty clearly played a role in her son's marriage, she explains. One day, it must have been—she stops to think—five years ago, they were walking down the street together in Clichy, where Nasser was living at the time. They walked past a middle-aged Moroccan couple with their daughter. Fadila took an immediate liking to the young woman, and said as much to her son. Nasser agreed. Shall I say something to them? suggested Fadila. Nasser nodded.

She turned around and went up to the threesome. She introduced herself and her son. They had a chat, and Fadila invited the parents and their daughter to have dinner at her place the following Saturday.

"I do it on purpose," she says. On purpose, to have them come up to her little room without delay, to show them that her only wealth is her energy and her dignity.

The dinner was a success (it is beyond Édith how five people could share a meal in that room). The two young people hit it off. Three months later they were married. The young woman was a secretary in Morocco, and her parents had a bit of property. They are fond of Nasser. They had a proper wedding. "In the church in Clichy," says Fadila, and before Édith can comment on the word church, she adds, "Is nice room in Clichy *mairie*, is very good for weddings."

She stands up and reaches for a large photograph in a cardboard frame next to the television. A radiant young woman in a white dress on the arm of a slim, slightly awkward young man.

"By the way," says Édith, "you told me you put the card with your name on it next to the television, but I don't see it."

"I put, is here."

Fadila picks up the card, which was indeed next to the television but face down, along with a small pile of papers which

Édith recognizes as the letters and words they have worked on together.

"You would see it better if you stood it up," says Édith, indicating a vertical plane with her right hand.

"Yes, is like children at school . . ."

"Children and grown-ups. If you see something every day, you end up remembering it."

Fadila stands the card against the side of the television. She has manners. The guest is always right.

But it is time to set off for Saint-Landry. They need at least ten minutes to get there on foot, and it would be better to be on time.

As they cross the courtyard, Édith observes how pleasant it is with the three trees. Fadila agrees. She sits down here whenever she can—she points to a stone bench next to the wall separating the courtyard from the neighboring apartments. Édith doesn't say anything, but all she can think of is the way Fadila comes down to this courtyard for fresh air when she is stifling at night. She must sit on this little bench in the dark.

Along the way, Fadila shows Édith around her neighborhood. She's been living in this arrondissement for eleven years. She points out the grocery shops, the Laundromat where she has her washing done by the kilo, the shops: "Is for children but is expensive"; "They has so nice shoes."

"It's a pleasant part of town," says Édith, who doesn't know this arrondissement very well.

"Yes, is only rich people. Is very calm and quiet."

They are not late on arriving in Saint-Landry but other candidates have come early, so Fadila is given the number 30. Gentlemen who look like retired seniors have everyone go and sit in a large room in the basement in rows of plastic chairs. Facing them are six wooden tables, against the wall.

It was here that Fadila tried years ago to learn to read. But the classes were held elsewhere, in a much smaller room. And the people Fadila had met back then are not here this evening.

The meeting is late getting started. The candidates continue to pour in. Everyone is chatting, although from time to time a woman with a chignon, wearing a straight plaid skirt, asks for silence. Édith notices worriedly that most of the candidates are young Filipino women, plus a dozen or so Moroccans of both sexes ("They is Moroccan," said Fadila), three black Africans, and a few Asians.

More candidates arrive and some benches are brought out. Then a group of young people who look like students come in: they must be the volunteer instructors.

And indeed they go and sit at the tables, facing the candidates. "Let's get started," says one of the older men in a loud voice.

The woman in the chignon knows what to expect from the Filipinos' level of language: she calls out the numbers in English, "Two! Sree!" in a caricature of an accent, until one of the Moroccans says, "Speak French, Madame!" As their numbers are called, the participants go to sit at one of the tables with a volunteer who helps them to fill out a form.

Fadila knows a few of the Moroccans. She points to one of the men in the group, in his forties, sitting next to a brown-haired woman. "Is not his wife," says Fadila, furious. His wife stayed behind in Morocco with the children, and now this is how he behaves, while the wife has to bring up the children all on her own, in addition to the housework.

"Is hard, children, when you is all alone."

"At least, thanks to the father, there's some money in the family," says Édith.

"Money is not everything," retorts Fadila, with one of those idiomatic expressions she uses from time to time.

When children grow up like this, she continues, only seeing

their father once a year, they don't know him, "is no respect, is no good relation."

The numbers are called, one by one. Number 15, number 16. Édith asks Fadila whether she would prefer to go to the interview alone or accompanied. Accompanied, opts Fadila, without hesitating. Clearly she has noticed that she is the only one in her particular situation, for when the manager walks by, she stops her and says, "I is coming with is lady teaching me to write. Is okay she come enrolment with me?" The woman has no problem with that. As soon as she is out of earshot Fadila leans closer to Édith and says, "Must to always telling truth, like that is no trouble after. I is always telling truth."

The fact remains that she is probably the oldest of all those who have come to enroll. She sits unmoving, slightly slumped on her chair, observing those around her. Fadila has that swarthy face with heavy eyelids, thin lips, and the impressive implacability often found in old women from a poor background, whatever the continent, as if age made them all alike. In fact, she looks much older than her sixty-four or sixty-five years. Which won't argue in her favor today.

Fadila's turn has come. Fate has it that she is interviewed by an exquisite young man, as friendly as can be. Fadila states her identity, her address, her telephone number. When he asks, "Are you married?" she replies fiercely, "No." Édith breaks in: "You're living alone now. But you have been married, you have children and grandchildren."

"And is children is granddaughters," adds Fadila. "I's old."

The young man asks her if she has any notions of reading or writing. She shakes her head and says, "No a lot." "Well, still," corrects Édith, "you can write your first and last name, and read a few things here and there."

Édith in turn—careful to do it in front of Fadila—asks whether it is true that there will not be room for all the candidates. The young man seems surprised. "We do have a lot of people this year," he says.

The classes will begin in a week, on the 14th, at the same time and place. They will call all the candidates beforehand to confirm their enrolment.

But no one calls Fadila. On the 13th, the evening before the first class, Édith calls to find out what is happening. A young woman answers; Édith does not recognize her voice, and she confirms that Fadila Amrani has not been accepted. The reason? She doesn't know. She is not familiar with the case.

Before telling Fadila, Édith calls other literacy centers she had located, which offer classes at the end of the afternoon. The only one that has a class at six P.M. is an association run by the *mairie,* the town hall of the sixteenth arrondissement. The classes are held at the *mairie* itself, it's not very far from Fadila's place, with a direct métro: it might work.

Enrolment has been closed since July, says a pleasant woman on the telephone, but very often people who have signed up drop out after a few weeks: Fadila can come and fill out a form, and they'll have a place for her as soon as someone drops out.

Édith explains that the reason she has been so late in calling is that she was counting on another literacy center, but that Fadila was turned down because of her age. "Do you think that might be a problem?"

The woman is not surprised. "Well, obviously, a young person can learn to read and write in two years, an older person takes ten years. These are people who have never learned how to learn. Some of them have never even held a pencil.

"But we won't exclude anyone because of their age. We are prepared to give everyone a chance."

Fadila does not seem surprised to find out that she has not

been accepted at Saint-Landry. It's a well-known fact in her milieu: "Is Filipinos they taking all the places."

The very next morning she goes to sign up at the *mairie* in the sixteenth arrondissement, where they do indeed put her on a waiting list, assuring her that they will contact her the moment a spot becomes available.

The likelihood seems slim. The prospect of resuming her lessons with Fadila leaves Édith with a weariness that merely serves to emphasize how much she had been counting on being relieved of her task.

14

F adila, however, when they meet the following week, says to Édith, "We is going on together you and me" with so much good grace and enthusiasm that Édith is moved. This is all about Fadila, but she doesn't seem either discouraged or skeptical.

Does she have the impression that she's made progress with Édith, that she's learned a lot? Or if she knows that she has learned very little, does it mean that for her even that very little is important? Does she prefer their private meetings to a class with others?

"Let's do some reading to start with today, if that's all right with you," says Édith.

On a sheet of paper she writes

RER C   *FADILA*
AMRANI   *RER B*
RER A   *LARBIT*

and hands the paper to Fadila: "These are all words that you know."

Fadila does not seem convinced. She looks at the sheet, immobile. All the same, as if moving a pawn in chess, she slides her index finger over to the word *AMRANI* and says, "That one, is Amrani." Then, taking heart, she points to *FADILA* and relaxes. "That one is me."

"It's your first name," says Édith. "That's good, you recognized it. But it's not you, you cannot say, 'It's me,' it's your first name, Fadila."

Before Fadila's eyes she writes *ME*: "This is the word me. Look, here you have the word *FADILA*, and this is the word *ME*: they're different. Do you understand?"

Apparently not altogether, for when Fadila points to *LARBIT*, she says, "Is Nasser."

"It's Nasser's name," says Édith, "the name you see on your telephone when he calls."

"Is Larbit."

"Exactly. There is the man who is your son, then there is his name. You know that it isn't the same thing."

Édith writes *NASSER*. "There's something special about this word. Do you see what it is?"

Fadila cannot tell.

"It's your son's first name, Nasser," says Édith. "Surely you know it."

She has Fadila pronounce the word, insists on the sibilants, writes the letter *S*—"a new letter"—and points out that there are two *S*'s in *NASSER*. It is the first time they have seen a double letter. Fadila copies the *S*, the two *S*'s, the name.

"Let's keep going," says Édith. She writes *AÏCHA*. "Your daughter's first name. Look: it begins and ends with a letter you know well."

They work on the A, the one that occurs twice in *FADILA*, twice in *AÏCHA*, twice in *AMRANI*, once in *NASSER* and *LARBIT*. Édith would have liked so much for Fadila to have noticed this. It's still too early.

The *A* is also what makes the difference between *RER A* and *RER B* or *RER C*. Édith reaches for a Paris transport map and shows her the spots, at the end of the RER lines, where it says A, B, or C: it's like a little label stuck to the line, so that you will know that this line is the A, this one the B, and this third one the C.

Fadila has often seen people looking at these little folders in the bus or on the métro, she says. She wondered what it was.

Édith points out the stations: each little white circle stands for an RER stop.

But she is afraid that all of this is far too abstract for someone who can hardly tell the difference between a name and a person, between a word and the thing itself.

She looks again on the internet, types *Teach illiterate adult to read* in the search engine. She has to know what is at stake, so that she can improve her own method.

There is a huge amount of information about the subject on-line. One particular site, *French as a foreign language*, is a veritable encyclopedia. In addition to the references it provides to all sorts of publications on learning, on theories about the learning process, on cognitive psychology, and on the contribution of neuroscience, among other things, it also offers a free audiovisual learning method in *333 reading games*, which looks extraordinary.

On other sites, pedagogues share their experience, and there are manuals for sale written by teachers who concluded that none of the existing textbooks are satisfactory. There are reports commissioned by international organizations, containing proposals for eliminating the inefficacy of adult illiteracy programs. Édith spends hours on these websites, entire evenings, taking pages of notes.

From a practical point of view she is relieved to see that, empirically, she has been doing just what is universally recommended. First and foremost the learning process has to have meaning; avoid working on information that has no significance (letters or syllables removed from any context); choose subject matter that represents a meaningful investment of time, such as first and last name. The teacher must not display any authoritarian or dogmatic behavior. Find out as much as possible about the student. Look for the single method best suited for each case.

Regarding theory, Édith reads dozens of times that motivation and commitment on the part of the student are fundamental, that the emotional side can play a decisive role (empathy of the initiator, quality of the relationship). There are fascinating pages describing everything that has come to light over the last century thanks to the contributions of psychology and, more recently, neuroscience. Experience—in other words, a lack of it, or gaps in experience—can be key in determining how easily a student will learn. Successive periods of learning have a lot to do with piling up the blocks. If the blocks at the foundation have been poorly placed, the pyramid cannot be built, it will collapse. Worse still, there are critical periods for certain stages of the learning process. Once these critical periods, and their particular dispositions, have elapsed, learning is no longer possible. Worst of all, if certain fundamental processes have not been learned when they could have been learned, other processes that depend on them (which are superimposed upon them) become impossible in turn, just as a pyramid cannot be built on a foundation that does not exist.

No one in the present day would dare to assert as aggressively as Luria did, at the height of the Soviet Union's influence, that illiterate adults from predominantly oral cultures can display deficiencies in the mechanisms of perception, generalization, abstraction, deduction, and inference; but nor can anyone rule out that possibility.

Édith stops right there. She needs to have at least a minimum of faith in a positive outcome. Because she will go on. Whatever her faith, she cannot abandon what she has begun. She cannot picture herself saying to Fadila: it's not going to work, let's drop it.

But there is one thing that is striking. On every site, in every story or analysis, no matter the approach or the method, the initial learning stage consists in showing a few letters and teaching the student to make basic combinations. And nowhere does it say that there are students who fail to assimilate this elementary ABC. The overall implication is that this basic knowledge is accessible to everyone—if there are difficulties, they will come later.

And this is where Édith has come a cropper, faced with such resistance to what is the basic cornerstone of learning. There are individuals to whom one can give an *F* and an *A* and who cannot combine them to make either *FA* or *AF*.

Édith has read hundreds of pages and nowhere is there any reference to such individuals. Well, there is, indirectly, in the two-fold conclusion that, on the one hand, all too often there are people who give up on their literacy classes—regrettably, since they were the ones who asked to take them; and on the other there are, invariably, programs on offer to the crowds of hopefuls that remain ineffective.

15

W hen Fadila comes in, her expression is inscrutable.
"Is everything all right?"
"Is no sleeping. Watching television all night. I seeing three programs is Special Correspondent, is shit. Is bullshit
all over, everywhere."

"But when you watch television like that at night aren't
there times when your eyes just start to close by themselves?
Don't you just drop off after a while?"

"Sometimes, yes. But sometimes is no sleeping all night. Is
good thing television working. I is all alone. If I switching off
television, I seeing things is no good. So I leave switched on. Is
not easy being alone."

The *Alphalire* method offered online on the French as a foreign language website, *lepointdufle*, is so well conceived, and
playful at the same time, in both its written and oral compo-
nents, as well as being full of imagery and not just graphic, that
Édith describes it enthusiastically to Fadila and suggests they
give it a try. On screen they can work without pencil and paper,
at least at the start; the student doesn't have to make the effort
to write, only recognize and identify, and compose syllables
with a click of the finger; it's a game.

Fadila is sitting at her usual place, on Édith's left, at the
table where they've become accustomed to working. But
instead of a sheet of paper, Édith places her little laptop computer between them. She notices at once that Fadila is sitting

well back from the table, deep in her chair. She does not lean toward the screen the way she would lean over the paper.

Édith shows her the first of the three hundred and thirty-three exercises, and she does not need to act cheerful: it really is a game.

They start with the five vowels. Each time they click on one of the letters, they hear a woman's voice saying the letter. The game consists in having the student point the cursor at a letter, then say the name of the letter out loud and, with a click, check whether or not they have given the right answer.

Édith has chosen the capital letters. She emphasizes once again to Fadila that she knows four out of the five vowels. "The fifth one is *u*, we'll deal with that one later. Let's start with the others." She shows Fadila how to move the cursor across the screen with her fingertip, how to put it on the chosen letter, and then how to click with a slight pressure of her finger to hear the name of the letter. "Go ahead, you'll see, it's easy."

Fadila shakes her head. She is glum. She keeps her back pressed against the chair, her hands on her thighs under the table. "Is computer I no doing," she says.

"Forget it's a computer. Just pretend it's a game. You know how to use a telephone: this is even simpler."

"I no doing," says Fadila again. "Is for young people. I'm be too old."

"Try it! Everyone can do it."

"I no can seeing on there," says Fadila, lifting her chin toward the screen. "I no see nothing."

"How can that be," says Édith. She points to the letter *A*. "You see the letter, here. You recognize it, no?"

Fadila goes on shaking her head. "I no can seeing." A stubborn child.

"Don't you want to try? Just once?"

The same sign language. No, no, no.

"Would you rather go on like before, with paper?"

"Yes."

"Fine," says Édith. "If you prefer. After all, in the old days before computers we didn't need them to learn how to read."

She will think about Fadila's refusal later. For the time being the main thing is to stay cheerful.

She closes the laptop, shoves it to one side, and reaches for the sheets and the felt-tips. On one sheet—comprising their entire fortune—are the words they have already seen:

FADILA   AMRANI
NASSER   LARBIT
AÏCHA
RER A
RER B
RER C

The time before, when Édith had added *AÏCHA* to the list of words Fadila knew, she had hoped Fadila would notice the dieresis above the I and ask her what these two dots were for. Now while she goes over the words again one by one, she hopes Fadila will say something about the dieresis. But no questions come.

So Édith points to the dieresis: this sign means anybody can recognize *AÏCHA* among the other words, she explains.

But apparently, it doesn't apply to everyone, as the minutes which follow make amply clear. At least not straight off, where Fadila is concerned.

Édith realizes that the problem is precisely that Fadila cannot learn such simple things with her first attempt, and, for lack of an explanation, she now knows that repetition, tedious repetition, will have to be one kind of solution.

She goes back to the letter *U*. They mustn't miss the opportunity to learn another letter.

"On the computer you saw that there are four letters you know . . ."

Fadila does not deny it. She does not repeat that she couldn't see anything on the screen.

While she is speaking, Édith writes *A, E, I, O*.

" . . . and there's one more, a new one, the *U*."

Some writing practice. Work on the *U*. Simplified writing: just a curve, no vertical serif on the right side. Fadila relaxes.

Édith notices that she still doesn't hold her pen properly.

Suddenly an idea springs to mind: "You know you've got nearly all the letters, now."

She writes the twenty-six letters of the alphabet on two lines and shows them one by one to Fadila. She doesn't question her. She draws a red circle around each of the letters they have already seen, affirming, "You already know this one very well," and only then does she ask, "Which one is this?"

Once again she can see there are varying degrees in Fadila's knowledge, and there is a major difference between recognizing and naming. Just because Fatima is familiar with a letter she doesn't necessarily know how to name it.

Still, they come up with fifteen red circles, fifteen letters that Fadila knows, to varying degrees.

"That's a lot, out of twenty-six," says Édith, jubilant.

She rewrites the twenty-six letters on a sheet of paper, and asks Fadila, once she is at home and relaxed, to pick out the ones that are familiar. "You can make a circle around it, or a square. Squares are easy to make."

She adds the gesture to her words, four lines. This brings back a memory from Luc's early childhood. The family pediatrician recommended the children undergo a series of tests offered by the Social Security, once they turned two and four.

Luc was four. The psychologist gave him a blank sheet of paper and a pencil: "Can you draw a square for me?" He sat there silent and motionless. Édith assumed he didn't know how. The woman said again, "Draw a square for me." So Luc, determined, said: "I'd rather draw a sun." And without waiting for her green light, he drew a huge sun, with S-shaped sunbeams, filling the entire page.

"It doesn't matter," said the psychologist. It really doesn't, is what Édith would have said.

Two days later she walked by Luc and saw he was drawing, and she asked, "Say, don't you want to draw a square?" And the little boy, as if he were fed up with all this obsession with squares, immediately drew a square, with four very confident pencil strokes.

Fadila watches as Édith puts away some of the boys' clothes that are lying around: shoes and trousers into the wardrobe, a parka onto the coatrack, a belt into a drawer. "Is always the mama she picking up everything," she says, sympathetically.

Édith and Gilles have a friend who has just lost his wife. The children are quite young still. Édith tells Fadila about it. The friend has assured them that everything is fine, he's gotten organized, but Édith wonders, in concrete terms, how he is getting on with their everyday life.

"When is mama dying, life is go all black." Fadila tells her again about her mother, about her own sorrow when she died. Édith says, dully, "She lived a long life, she was old."

"Yes," nods Fadila. "Is sixty."

Her mother died a gentle death, the kind she would like to have, she says. She was in Casablanca, with her granddaughter Aïcha, who was twenty at the time and had been married for a while already. She was fine. She was to have left a few days earlier to go back to be with Fadila, with whom she was living in Rabat, but Aïcha had insisted she stay on a bit longer until her mother-in-law came back from Mecca "with things for her."

Fadila's mother had agreed to postpone her departure. The "hadja" came home, told them all about her pilgrimage, and they listened. Everyone had dinner and went to bed. The grandmother had planned to leave the next morning. She got up at dawn and said her prayer. But when she went to get dressed, she couldn't. She went to rouse Aïcha, and Aïcha realized something was wrong. They fussed over her. "Don't worry," said the grandmother, "I'm dying." She lay down, said her prayers, very calmly, and died.

Fadila's great regret is that they were not able to reach her in time for her to see her mother again before the burial. In Islam the burial takes place very soon after death. "If is die in the morning, has to burying before evening prayer." She knows that it is different for Christians, that they let a few days go by. "Is be sure the person is really dead," she says, evoking a fear that Édith knew, from her reading, had been prevalent in bygone eras, but which seemed to have disappeared in their own.

"What sort of work did you do in Rabat?"

Fadila had been the housekeeper for a French couple with three children. People who ran a café. "Is Jewish, but is very nice," she says. She raised their children. She spent more than twelve hours a day with this family, and that is why she is grateful to her own mother for having come to keep house for her and take care of the children while they were little.

"Your daughters got married very young," says Édith.

"No. Aïcha is eighteen, Zora seventeen."

"That's not exactly old. You said you found it so hard, getting married when you were still a girl—wouldn't you have preferred for them to wait a bit?"

"Girls is have to getting married young," says Fadila firmly, "otherwise is going around with boys, is no good."

"You were twenty-five when you were on your own with your children and went to work in Rabat?"

"Twenty."

"You were twenty and you'd already been married three times?"

"No, is third is after, in Rabat. I'm no luck with husbands."
She changes her tone: "Is ironing to do. Gotta go."

However willingly she speaks of her mother, she will only
talk about her husbands if Édith asks her about them, and then
she quickly changes the subject.

16

Ramadan has begun. Fadila is in a bad mood. She works fewer hours, and leaves earlier. She has to finish cooking before breaking the fast, which is set for seven in the evening these days. And the ritual meal takes a long time to prepare. She really has no time at all for reading and writing.

One morning she calls to say she won't be coming this Tuesday. She had an upset stomach all night. "Is lady giving me Ramadan cakes is making someone in Morocco."

Cakes that keep one awake all night long, from the country where Fadila cannot go without being sick.

The following week, her upset stomach is better, so she comes to do the ironing. But she is still in a black mood. Her back aches. Every year it's the same thing, she says. She cannot stand fasting.

Édith asks Fadila whether, given the fact that sick people are exempt from fasting, and that not being able to drink anything makes her sick, she could not exempt herself from fasting, or at least allow herself to drink. Fadila does not grasp this casuistry, is shocked, even: "I no sick, since I working. If you working, you no sick!"

It is Fadila who comes, once she has finished ironing, to sit by Édith and say, "We going writing a little today?"

Édith asks her to write her first and last names. She no longer watches while she does it. It has been a long time since she had to guide her hand.

Fadila puts down her felt-tip and sits up straight. She wrote *FADILFADIL* and below that, *MRANI*. Édith is bewildered.

"You wrote *FADILA* twice?"

"Yes," she replies, cheerfully, as if she were saying, "Why not?"

Édith points out that there is a letter missing from *FADIL*, and a letter missing from *MRANI*. Fadila cannot see which one.

"Both times it's the *A*."

This seems to amuse Fadila.

Édith writes slowly there before her: *AMRANI*. Just below that, Fadila writes *AMRAI*. Édith points out that there is a letter missing. Fadila cannot see which one.

"The *N*," says Édith.

Fadila starts over. This time she writes *AMRNI*. Same observation, letter missing. Same fog, she cannot find it.

"That's the one that's missing," says Édith, pointing with her finger.

"Ah, the *A*," says Fadila, identifying it at last.

They move on to reading. Édith writes *RER B*. Fadila reads *RER C*. *LARBIT*: she recognizes it. *RER C*: she reads *RER A*. *NASSER*: she cannot.

"You know, is very difficult," she says.

Édith suddenly feels so helpless, that she has to find a trick, a magic formula, a mantra. If only Fadila could grasp that words are made up of syllables, she thinks, with a sort of despair, as if she were squeezing a lucky charm, the overall difficulty would be transformed into tiny little efforts. Syllables are tiny, very simple little words.

She divides *FADILA* into three, circles the *FA*, then the *DI*, then the *LA*. "We're going to try a little exercise with your first name, the word you know best. At the same time as you write *FA*, you will say *fa*, and then *di* when you write *DI*, then *la* when you write *LA*."

You have your eyes, your ears, and your mouth. You learn from all sides. If you say what you write that's one way of absorbing it. It is bound to work.

But Fadila must think it's ridiculous, she doesn't follow. Or else, thinks Édith, the way we pronounce the word in French must seem light years away from what she knows of her first name. For a moment Édith imagines someone asking her to write her first name in Arabic, using Arabic letters, in other words, with no capital or final *h*. It would be a transcription. A very abstract process: you change the word before putting it down in writing in unfamiliar signs. It's hard, very hard.

But the following Tuesday Fadila writes *AMRANI* perfectly, first try. Édith squeezes her in her arms.

She remembers the first thing Fadila wrote for her, that little scribble of messy, unrecognizable signs: it's absolutely clear that they've made considerable headway in seven months. Considerable headway with nothing at all.

And that is the day, the last in the month, when Fadila leaves with her paycheck. As she is preparing to endorse the check on the back with her usual zigzag, Édith suggests she try signing her name instead. You cannot just change your signature like that, retorts Fadila; you have to warn the bank. Maybe she knows this because she told her branch office that one day she would sign her name?

Édith has left herself a reminder at the end of the table, a piece of cardboard on which she has written in big fat letters: *LAUNDRY*. She mustn't forget to take out a load she started a while ago and hang it up to dry.

Fadila picks up the piece of cardboard: "What's this?" she asks.

"Laundry," says Édith. And she shows Fadila that she already knows the *L*, the *A*, the *U*, the *N*, the *D*, and the *R*. "The only one that's new is the *Y*. It's not too difficult."

"Have to learning this word, too," says Fadila, and Édith adds *LAUNDRY* to their treasure.

The doorbell rings. It is Aïcha who has come to visit her mother.

"I won't offer you any coffee because of Ramadan," says Édith.

"It's as if you had," answers Aïcha.

They go and sit in the kitchen. Before long the tone of their voices becomes animated. Aïcha comes over to Édith at her work desk and asks her for a sheet of paper.

"I'm showing her that letters are easy," she says.

"It's easy when you know how to write," says Édith. "You've known for a long time, you went to school."

"Yes, I finished high school. I didn't pass my final exams, but at least I sat them. I started school at five."

17

Two days later Édith runs into Aïcha again at the post office.

"I wanted to ask you something, actually," she says. "Could you work with your mother a bit on her reading and writing? She's not spending enough time on it. She should do a bit every day."

"She'll never agree." Aïcha is adamant. "With me? Acting as teacher? No use even suggesting it to her."

They walk a short ways down the street together.

"She's not an easy person," says Aïcha. "We're getting along at the moment, but there have been other times . . . Poor woman, it's no wonder, with the life she's had."

Édith grabs the line she's been thrown.

"She was married three times, and not one of the marriages worked out?"

"Married, married . . . The second time, she was sold."

It was her father who arranged it. Fadila had just left her first husband, the year she turned fifteen. She went back to her parents. Her father had no intention of supporting her. He had heard that in Casablanca there was a rich man looking for a second wife. The man had been married for a long time and had no children, so he'd struck a bargain with his wife: he'd take a second wife, and once she had given him a son and a daughter—a son for him, a daughter for his wife—he would repudiate her.

"My mother had no choice," says Aïcha. "But what her father

didn't know at the time he was concluding his business was that she was pregnant with a second child. She hadn't told anyone about it because she was afraid it might prevent her from getting a divorce."

She complied with her father's demands, and went to Casablanca, to the house of the childless couple. "She couldn't understand a thing. She didn't speak Arabic, all she knew was Berber."

They found out she was expecting. It didn't really matter, but it did complicate things somewhat. The child was born three months after Fadila arrived in the home of the rich man, so no one would believe that he was the father.

"The child was Zora," says Aïcha. "My sister and I are true sisters. Same father, same mother."

As for the issue of paternity, it was easy to fix. They waited six months before declaring the birth. And of course Zora was declared as being the daughter of the man in whose house she was born.

The woman in want of a child now had her daughter, but they still needed a son. They did not wait long, Fadila fell pregnant again and a boy was born.

"A successful purchase," says Édith. "The couple must have been pleased."

"Yes and no," winces Aïcha. "The man, yes, the woman, no."

The wife reminded her husband of the terms of their agreement: You've had your son, I've got my daughter, we agreed, now you send Fadila away.

"But the thing was, the husband didn't want to send her away," laughs Aïcha. "My mother was a very beautiful woman, she was seventeen, he found her rather to his liking. He told his wife he had changed his mind."

"And then?"

"And then the first wife poisoned my mother. Just like in some story from a harem. It was a close call."

Fadila's mother had done everything she could to oppose the contract her husband had made. She had a brother in Casablanca so she stayed with him as often as possible, in order to be in touch with her daughter. You cannot stop a mother from visiting her child.

"So she was the one who brought you up, your grand-mother?"

"In addition to everything else, yes. She had me with her day and night. When she moved in with her brother in Casablanca, she took me there, too."

One Sunday, the rich man's wife told Fadila that she and her husband were going out for the day. "You stay here, your lunch is ready," she said to Fadila. When they left they locked the door.

Just by chance, that same afternoon Fadila's mother came to visit her daughter. She found the door locked. She knocked.

"You know what it's like back there," says Aïcha, "the houses so close together, everyone knows everyone else's business." The neighbors came out: "They've gone out." "And my daughter, too?" "No, your daughter stayed behind."

Through the door Fadila's mother could hear someone moaning. She sensed something was wrong.

She set off at a run to fetch her brother, and they came back together. The brother broke down the door. They found Fadila in a very bad way and took her to the hospital.

"My mother never set foot in that house again," says Aïcha. "At least the poisoning enabled her to get away from those people. A man who kept her there to sleep with her and nothing else; a woman who hated her. Her own children in the same house and she didn't even have the right to treat them as her own . . ."

Fadila didn't stop there, she sued the couple for fraudulent declaration of birth and attempted murder.

"The lawsuit took forever, it took the judges eight years to hand down their decision," says Aïcha. "The couple won. They had bought everyone—all the neighbors who could testify, the lawyers, the judges."

In the meantime Fadila had to find work. That was when she went to stay in Rabat with her mother and Aïcha, and went into service for "the very nice Jews."

"I thought she had raised three children in Rabat?" says Édith.

"The couple kept Zora and Khaled. My mother had two more children after them."

Édith keeps her surprise to herself. Fadila has never breathed a word about Khaled. It would be an understatement to say she talks about Nasser, calling him her son, she never calls him anything but *my son*. Moreover, she has always insisted she has three children; now Aïcha is talking about five.

"In Rabat she met a man she liked, and she got pregnant again," continues Aïcha.

"I'm glad to hear she finally met a man she was in love with," says Édith tenderly, while working out that Fadila must not have been much older than twenty.

"Another bastard. She loved him all right, but he was married."

"Did he take her as his second wife, too, then?"

"In a manner of speaking."

"Did he marry her?"

"Only a religious marriage. I remember, he used to come and spend the night at our place two or three times a week."

Nasser was born soon after. By then Fadila's father's patience was at its limit, and he demanded that Fadila's mother return to the marital home. His wife refused and stayed in Rabat with her daughter. Her husband got a divorce and remarried.

"Basically Nasser was the first of her children she was able to bring up herself," comments Édith.

"He was the only one."

For Fadila was pregnant again, and when the man she loved found out, he left her. "I told you, a bastard." The fifth child was born, a third son, but he died very young.

"I know that Zora married young, that she has several children, that she lives in Aubervilliers," says Édith. "And Khaled, what became of him? Does he live in Morocco?"

Aïcha tells her that he and Zora had everything they needed. Édith understands this to mean, Unlike me. "They were educated at the French Mission. Khaled has a technical degree."

"Were their adoptive parents good to them?"

"Of course they were. They spoiled them."

Until Khaled, at fifteen, came upon the family booklet and discovered there were two names on the line that said *Mother*, both for him and his sister. He asked about it. They lied to him. He would not give up, and he found out that his mother was not the woman who had brought him up.

"It drove him crazy. He began to go off the rails. He made life impossible for his adoptive mother."

He began to live on the edge; he drank, ended up in prison. Aïcha falls silent for a moment.

As for Zora, she continues, not only did she find out that she was not the daughter of the woman she had always believed was her mother, but also that the man she thought was her father was not her father either. She got married very quickly.

"You can see why my mother loves her son so much," says Aïcha. "He's the only one of her children who grew up in her home."

Édith notices that Aïcha says *her son*. Not my brother, or even my half-brother.

"I get the impression that your grandmother was quite a person."

"My grandmother?" Aïcha beams. "She was a fabulous woman. She died in my house, you know."

"I know. Your mother loved her so much."

"And as for my grandmother: how she loved her daughter! My mother hasn't been very lucky in life, but at least she's had that. She was everything to her mother."

18

The literacy center at the *mairie* of the sixteenth arrondissement has not called back. Édith decides to look into it. They confirm that Madame Amrani is indeed on a waiting list, but nothing has opened up, they tell her. The friendly lady had been so sure, however, back in September. "People who enroll frequently give up quite soon": Édith remembers what she said, word for word.

She pictures a red dot next to the name Amrani on the waiting list. Perhaps they're not in any hurry, in this center either, to make room for an illiterate Moroccan woman who's already old.

One day instead of *FADILA* she writes *FANILA*. Where did this *N* come from, a letter she doesn't like and hardly knows, instead of the *D* which she knows and writes very well?

Another time she writes *FADI* very slowly then stops: "I forgetting."

"Take your time. It will come back."

She adds an *M* then shakes her head. "I no doing good. I'm so tired."

"On days when you're tired, you don't work as well, that's normal."

Édith wouldn't like her to give up just when she's failed, so she places before her a sheet where she had already written her first name on an earlier occasion, and asks her to copy it. Fadila writes a tiny crooked *FADILA*, a sickly scrawl. "I forgetting. You know, I'm old."

"No you're not. You've been doing really great," says Édith. She needs to hear these words herself, too.

"You just have to write a little bit every day. It's the same thing for everyone, you know, if you don't keep something going, you forget it."

The following Tuesday, while Fadila is writing her name, Édith gets up and goes to open a letter, so that she won't be watching Fadila. She has sometimes gotten the impression that it makes things easier for Fadila if she isn't being watched.

Fadila hesitates, writes, stops. Édith comes to have a look. She has written *AMRIA*. The beginning of *AMRANI*, plus two letters from the end of *FADILA*: confusion, forgetfulness. How is Édith to understand such a fragile capacity for memorization? Could she have lost, in the space of two weeks, something she used to manage straight off the bat?

Édith is dismayed. She tries not to show it.

"This here is your name, *AMRANI*. The beginning is right, but the end, not quite. Can you put your first name in front?"

Fadila writes *ADIL*, the heart of the word, minus the beginning and the end. Édith says nothing and adds an *F* at the beginning and an *A* at the end.

Fadila points to the *A*: "I forgetting that one again."

"It's strange, don't you think? A letter you know so well. Do you remember what it is called?"

"*A*."

"Exactly," says Édith.

She opens the textbook to the page where the entire alphabet is printed. "You see, it's the first letter." She points to the *A*'s she finds, here and there: "At the end of *FADILA*, at the beginning of *AMRANI*, at the beginning and the end of *AÏCHA*—do you see them?"

"Is everywhere," says Fadila, not really answering.

*

She rarely comes on days just to work on her reading. She blames fatigue, insomnia, worries.

Mid-November, the cold weather has started. Her ankle hurts. An old fracture, the pain comes back again every winter. Like something sharp piercing her leg, she says.

Gilles has persuaded Édith to change her email program, to give up Orange and switch to Thunderbird. The names of the files and the functions are different, the icons are different, the maneuvers are different. Édith can tell that Thunderbird is indeed an improvement in terms of flexibility, capacity, and the possibilities available. But she had other things to do that evening, and what Gilles is showing her has upset her rhythm. She doesn't understand what he is saying. He is clicking and typing ten times too fast for her. He wants her to remember everything straight off, but she's someone who always needs to put things into words in order to memorize them. She moans, and he scolds, "Stop being childish."

She thinks of Fadila. Tonight Édith is being asked to enter a mental world that is unfamiliar; to discover signs, a language, a system of symbols that are disconcerting. It's going too fast. She is lost. She feels too old. She can't cope. And yet she knows it will be to her benefit, and she's prepared to make an effort. It's all so complicated, so tiresome.

She is also perfectly aware that the effort she is being asked to make is nowhere near as great as what she regularly expects from Fadila. Her instructor is speaking to her in her native language, and affectionately. She has been using computers for years. The adjustment she is being asked to make is marginal, and clearly defined.

"We gotta do is something different," says Fadila.

Édith would like nothing better. She writes, then reads, *LAUNDRY*. "Do you remember?" Fadila copies out the word.

Édith has her write the first letter on her own, *L*, and then next to it, the second one, *A*. She points to *LA* and asks her, "What does that make, *L* and *A*?"

"*Fa*," says Fadila.

She takes her homework sheets with her. She almost never brings them back. And every time she says the same thing: "I doing a lot but forgetting the paper." "I forgetting the paper but is doing a lot." "I doing everything but is leaving paper at Zora's house."

One days Édith suspects she is making things up, so she says, neutrally, "It doesn't matter if you don't bring the paper back. What does matter is that you worked. I can tell when you've been practicing. Because it goes well."

And the more time goes by, the more often Fadila says, straight out, "I no doing writing. I'm too tired."

Martin had a little time off at the beginning of the afternoon. One of his teachers was absent, and there was a free period. He called his paternal grandmother, who lives two métro stops from the lycée, and invited himself to lunch at her place.

He told his mother the story when he got home. Fadila overheard, and paused in her ironing: "Is nice boy, Martin. Is my grandchildren they never coming to see me. They saying, 'Why you no coming my house?' I'm old, I no have car, they wanting me go see them? No is possible!"

"It's nice at least that they invite you."

"Nice? Is no nice! Sometimes is making sad, I start crying."

"You mustn't cry, Fadila."

"Is not me crying, is my heart."

19

Fadila's got the numbers down, more or less. She knows how to read them and use them. Writing is another matter, and memorizing them harder still.

They work on Fadila's telephone number and the electronic code for the entrance to her building, B862.

Fadila knows her code, she uses it every day. She can even write it from memory from time to time, with her own special way of making the 2.

She has greater difficulty with the telephone number. She still doesn't know it by heart. She copies it without too much effort, but certain numbers give her a hard time, the 2, 4, 5, and 7.

The hardest of all is the 4. Édith guides her hand and breaks the gesture into three consecutive movements corresponding to the three pencil strokes. She says, just as she had to the children, "It looks like a little chair."

"I am sure you can write the beginning of your telephone number from memory," she ventures.

Fadila writes 01, then an illegible little sign, a sort of poorly made K. Édith asks her to take a good look at the 4. Fadila gives it a rounded back. Édith mimes the three pencil strokes: there is no curve to a 4, only three straight lines: the first two must be drawn without lifting the pen, and then the third one, this time after lifting the pen. Fadila does a series of impeccable 4's.

From memory she writes *01 40.* The *4* is perfect. Édith claps her hands.

"Is easy," says Fadila, and for the twentieth time, Édith assures her that writing letters can be just as easy.

She has her work on the next two digits from her telephone number, the *7* and the *2.* Two digits that give her trouble.

After five minutes Fadila lays down her pen. "That's enough for today," she says, coming out as she does from time to time with a perfect expression, perfectly pronounced.

She has a glum expression on her face. Her telephone line has been cut. She doesn't understand why, she's never been late with her payments.

She has brought her latest bill with her. She asks Édith to call France Télécom.

Over the phone, the representative does not take long to find the problem. France Télécom didn't cut the line; rather, Fadila herself asked to change carriers.

Édith relays this information to Fadila, and she exclaims, "Ah, is Nassima!" Nassima, her cousin, persuaded her to change carriers so she would have "free telephone." Nassima's husband said he would take care of it, over the internet. End result: Fadila has no more phone.

She fulminates. "I swearing, Nassima no do nothing only stupid things."

Once again she takes the measure of what it has cost her not to know how to read and write. "You is right making me go to school," she says to Édith.

Things are looking better. Her daughter-in-law has cancelled, in writing, her contract with the "feebok" and signed her up again with France Télécom. Her line is working again. It takes a while for Édith to understand that "feebok" is "freebox," the miracle system that allows you to make phone calls, watch television, and have internet access all for next to nothing.

"Is not only me is telephone no working," says Fadila. It's an obvious scam. It costs €30 to sign up. To cancel the contract you have to pay €100. Everyone signs up and then cancels, and the "feebok" rakes in a tidy sum. "If ever I finding TV reporter, I no care, I tell him."

She brings in a sheet of paper with her own work on numbers. Her telephone number, to be precise. "Is okay, the number?" she asks.

Yes and no. Yes, with the exception that the 2 is still a 9 facing the wrong way, and of the two 7's, one is correct and the other is backwards.

It looks as if all Fadila is doing, still, is copying, without knowing what the numbers actually stand for: it's more like drawing (approximate, clumsy) than reading. Édith makes her work on the 2, which she has so much trouble with, and the 7, which doesn't seem as hard.

But the following Tuesday, it's the other way round: Fadila cannot write the 7, whereas she gets the 2 right first try.

"I having to learning telephone numbers is my children," she says.

"Learn, learn." Édith points out that most people have a little notebook with an index where they list the numbers they need.

The index: this could be a way to study the letters, the initials and the very purpose of setting them apart like that. Édith has an unused address book. She has Fadila copy out *AÏCHA* under *A*, *NASSER* under *N*. "Do you want to learn Zora?"

"Is you writing."

"Look, this is the *Z*, the last letter, on the last page."

No sooner has she written *ZORA* than Fadila gets up, leaving the address book on the table. Édith hands it to her: "It's for you."

"What is do if I taking?" asks Fadila. "I no doing nothing."

"What you can do," says Édith, who would like to mobilize Fadila's family if she can, "is to ask your children, and other people around you, to write their name and telephone number in the notebook, on the right page."

"All right," says Fadila. "Give it to me."

But Édith gets the impression she has taken it out of politeness, not to refuse a gift twice.

Fadila overhears Édith on the telephone, first protesting, then suddenly silent. Finally she hangs up and just stands there, lost in thought.

She goes over to her: "Is something wrong?"

Yes, explains Édith. Something to do with her work. A thief. A publisher who had her do a long translation, and now he won't pay her. A brazen liar.

"Is worse things than that," says Fadila, reassured. "Is getting sick and no getting better, is somebody dying . . ."

In theory she can write the first eight digits of her telephone number from memory, 01 40 72 75, but in practice it's never a given. Sometimes she forgets the zero at the beginning, or the zero in the fourth position. And yet that zero, of all the numbers, is the one that gives her the least trouble, both to identify and to write.

Which all goes to make for a very small gain. But now Fadila will be able to take down a number over the phone. Édith remembers how one day she had to leave a number on Fadila's answering machine, not her home number: she carefully said one digit after the other and asked her to call back. Fadila had not returned the call, and later she explained that as she did not know how to write down a number, she could not use it.

*

No, this Tuesday she won't do any reading. She has a headache. She has caught cold. She freezes at night in her little room. It's not that she doesn't have any heating: her son has given her an electric radiator. But the device doesn't have a thermostat, so if she switches it on when she goes to bed, even on the lowest temperature, after a few hours she is suffocating. So she sleeps without the heat on.

What about the address book where she was going to have her family write their numbers? She doesn't know where she's put it. She showed it to her daughter-in-law, she must have left it at her place.

Luc comes home from school. On his way to leave his schoolbag in his room he says hello to Fadila, who is ironing.

Édith didn't notice. But Fadila comes to her and says: "Is beautiful boy, Luc, I being very happy. Even if isn't my kid is making me very happy. I asking God for good health for him always. Your children is very nice. They showing respect, they combing their hair. Some children is wearing something here (she pinches her ear), or here (she pinches her nostrils), is trousers dragging in cat wee, is make me furious, not you?"

C hristmas? No, she didn't have a good time. She would rather not talk about it.

But then she says, "You think is normal is old woman all alone Christmas Eve? Is not even go the dinner with her family?"

All too often she is tired, hasn't got time, doesn't feel like it; she won't work with Édith that day.

Sometimes just before leaving she asks hastily for some homework; Édith gets the impression it is just to make her teacher happy. It's not as if she brings the worksheet back with her; she just says, "next time."

Fadila must have been very disappointed not to have been admitted to any of the literacy courses. She must have seen this as a sign that no one thought she was even capable of learning how to read. Édith cannot persuade her to get back into a more sustained work rhythm. It's as if Fadila has lost faith.

One day by chance Édith runs into her cousin, Sara, on the rue de Rennes; that long mane of red hair, as she stands unlocking her bike, is unmistakable. Édith goes up to her and relates her difficulties with Fadila, and her own doubts about her abilities as a teacher.

"You know," says Sara as she straddles her bike, "it's very rare that people with a background like your lady's really manage to learn to read and write. They may learn to write their name, or read a few useful everyday words, the ones they see in the street or in the shops, the ones they need to fill in a form for sick leave. But to get to the point where they can read a book, or even the newspaper, that would be exceptional."

It's not the best time to begin, either, at the end of the day, when everyone else has finished work. But Fadila is no longer willing to start the lesson upon arrival. Édith wonders if it isn't simply that in the evening she can blame the time of day or her fatigue to get the lesson over with more quickly, or even postpone it until another time.

Her first name: she hesitates. She writes *FADI* then stops. Édith tries to help her find what is wrong. "Is just one number missing," says Fadila. "I know is five."

Édith hasn't got the heart to tell her that in this case it is letters, not numbers, and that there aren't five, but six altogether. She adds *LA* to *FADI* and says, "The *L* and the *A*." But there are no clear signs that Fadila has understood, or that her analytical approach is the right one.

She remembers—why just now?—how at the very beginning she had started off by separating vowels from consonants, the former were red, the latter green . . . The luxury of a rich person. An idiotic rich person.

They read the words Fadila knows. *LARBIT*: Fadila initially says Nasser. (In the beginning she always hurries, answering at random; then she gets hold of herself, and makes fewer mistakes.) *AÏCHA*: she reads *Fadila*. *FADILA*: she says, "Is me."

Édith writes *ME* for her: "Here, this is me." Fadila laughs, points to *FADILA*, she's understood: "Is my name."

"That's right," says Édith. "Good, your reading is fine, let's learn a new word."

Fadila laughs: "You thinking is fine? Is no fine at all!"

"Let's look at a new word," says Édith again. "*Madame.* You know that you are Madame Amrani. You have *Madame Amrani* on the letters you get. Perhaps you have a letter in your handbag right now?"

Fadila always has her business mail with her, so she takes out an envelope. Édith circles *Madame* with a pencil. She writes it in capital letters. Fadila copies out the word easily.

"Perfect," says Édith. "Now you add your name, and you'll get Madame Amrani."

She has something in mind. She would like to see if when she writes *AMRANI* after *MADAME*, Fadila will lop off the initial *A*, the way she often does when she writes it after *FADILA.*

Yes and no. She begins by writing *MRA*, then she inserts the *A* at the beginning and says, "Is not a lotta room," and she finishes the name by adding *NI* to the end.

While she watches, Édith adds the words *ME* and *MADAME* to their treasure chest.

The experts are unanimous in affirming that it is easier to learn something when it is obvious that it will be useful: Édith continues to work on Fadila's mailing address.

She asks Fadila for another envelope with her name on it. With the pencil she underlines *Madame Fadila Amrani*:

"These three words you already know. Let's look at what comes next."

She points to the address, on its line, 62 rue de Laborde, 75008 Paris, and she explains each element of the address in turn, writing *RUE* in large letters for Fadila.

"You've known the *R* for a long time now, you have it in *RER*, both here and here. The *E* is the letter in the middle of *RER*. We saw *U* not long ago, and you managed to write it right away. This little word, *RUE*, is on nearly every envelope, you'll see."

The day's mail is on the table. Édith takes three envelopes addressed to her and shows the word to Fadila on each of them.

Fadila writes it very well, right from the start.

"I already know is recognizing name on my letters," she says.

Since she seems to be fairly cheerful this evening, before she leaves Édith asks her to write her first and last name from memory. She writes *ADIRA AMRNNI*.

Édith corrects her and asks her to start over. Fadila writes *AFDILA AMRLANI*.

Fleetingly Édith wonders how many different combinations one can obtain from the letters that go to make up *Fadila Amrani*.

"Today is catastrophe," says Fadila.

There are a dozen or more Christmas cards on the dresser in the entrance. "Is everyone they writing you like this?" she asks.

"To my family and me, yes. People wishing us a happy new year."

"To me no one is writing. Not one person."

Perhaps that is because Muslim new year does not come at the same time, mumbles Édith. Fadila doesn't understand: "Is new year, is same for everyone. For us is same. New year day is new year day."

Edith's boys are sad to see how bitter Fadila is, so they send her very affectionate wishes, on a card featuring some Iznik pottery. Édith and Gilles also sign the card.

A few days later Fadila shows up, very moved, with a pile of letters that she thrusts into Édith's hands. In the pile is their Christmas card.

"Ah, you got it."

"Yes, I go asking Madame Aubin, is tell me is very nice."

But that is not what she wanted to show Édith: in the pile there is a letter from Free telling her to pay for the freebox subscription which she had already cancelled several weeks earlier. Once Édith had heard about the cancellation she told Fadila not to send any money to Free anymore. And Fadila's daughter-in-law had also written to the carrier in response to a bill that came after the cancellation, to remind them that she had cancelled the subscription.

The letter from Free that Fadila has brought is not an order to pay, as she feared, but an answer to her daughter-in-law's letter: the carrier is asking for all the references, name and address of the subscriber, contract number, and so on.

Édith sums up the letter for Fadila, who bursts into tears. She tries to console her, saying, "It's nothing serious, we'll give them their references," but to no avail. Fadila weeps like someone who is at the end of her rope, who does not know how to defend herself, who is afraid she will have to pay something, yet again.

She wipes her eyes, raises her chin: "I showing letter to Nasser, is giving me back like this (an abrupt gesture), is saying no have time. He supposed to explaining me like you. Is my son! Why he saying he no has time?"

21

É dith has added the word *RUE* to their treasure chest. She shows Fadila how the list is getting longer, and she has her read a few of the words she knows. She asks her to take her time before speaking, to take a very good look first.

Fadila recognizes *RUE* (or almost: she says, "Is the street.") She reads *NASSER*, *LARBIT*, and *AÏCHA* correctly.

She can copy out *RUE DE LABORDE* without any difficulty. But when it comes to writing her full name from memory, she warns Édith that she can't do it anymore, she used to know but now it's gone. She writes *FADIA AMRLANI*.

Progress in reading, regression in writing: Édith finds it hard to understand. But she doesn't say anything. She draws a long rectangle on a sheet of paper, and inside it she writes:

MADAME FADILA AMRANI
RUE DE LABORDE

"Your street number, what was it again?"
"62."
"Go ahead, write it down."
She does not ask Fadila where she should put the number, she knows that it won't be obvious her, and she doesn't want to give her a trick question. She points to the spot and Fadila writes *62*, with a well-made *6* and a backwards *2*.

A building in Mecca has collapsed, killing seventy pilgrims.

Two days later, two hundred and fifty people die suffocated in a stampede of the kind which occur regularly around the Black Stone.

"You seeing what is happen in Mecca?" asks Fadila gravely.

"I saw, yes," says Édith.

Fadila, in a different tone, says resentfully, "Is some people they going Mecca four-five times!"

Édith cannot see what is wrong with that. Fadila explains, furious: "Is Koran saying must going Mecca one time. You think is normal is going Mecca four-five times instead to give money to people who no have money?"

Fadila needs a statement of what she was paid the previous year. There is a huge mess in Gilles' filing cabinet. Édith cannot find the papers she needs.

"My husband is a good man," she says, "but putting things away is not his thing."

After a pause, Fadila adds, "Is all men they the same."

"No, not all of them. I assure you."

"Is men they no making effort putting things away," insists Fadila. "Is no trying, ever."

"Can you write something besides your name, all on your own? *RER*, for example? Or *LARBIT*, which you see on your phone a lot?"

"No," says Fadila.

Perhaps reading does not make her as anxious. Fadila can more or less make out *RER A*, *RER B*, and *RER C*. Édith reminds her that *A*, *B*, and *C* are the first three letters of the alphabet. She opens the manual and asks Fadila to find them. "At the top," she says.

She would like Fadila to identify a few letters at last, particularly the initial letters of words. She shows her on their treasure chest list how *A* is found at the beginning of *AMRANI* and

AÏCHA, but nowhere else; how *LARBIT* and *LAUNDRY* both begin with an *L*, and *MADAME* and *ME* both begin with *M*. It is a tool for telling words apart, easy to use.

She gets the impression that Fadila understands the principle, but does not have the means to put it into practice. While she may know these few letters, she does not know them well enough to say their names or even the sound they make.

With the numbers there has been some progress—at least insofar as reading them is concerned. Fadila can read as far as 34. After that—go figure—she hesitates.

Édith congratulates her. Fadila tells her that she has been trying on her own lately. Trusting herself enough to read the price on items in the shops. "Before, in shop, I always asking other people. Now is no more asking."

Édith apologizes, this Tuesday she can hardly speak. She can't even smile. She has spent the morning at the dentist's, she's had a tooth pulled and the anesthesia is still paralyzing half her jaw.

"Is good, is no more hurting," says Fadila. "When tooth is come out, is no more hurting."

Which leads Édith to conclude that Fadila does not know that there are other ways to deal with a bad tooth besides pulling it, or merely waiting for it to fall out; one can have it treated, for example.

22

Fadila is coughing. From her bag she takes a bottle of syrup they sold her at the pharmacy: "Is no working at all."

Édith has to agree: "Cough syrup doesn't do any good. Only in France would they try to convince you otherwise. No, you know what works for a cough? Suppositories. You know what that is?"

Fadila makes a face: "I no like."

"That's as may be," says Édith, "But it's what works the best."

Fadila looks at her, a twinkle in her eye.

"You know what we are doing in Morocco?" she begins, then, "No, I no can say."

She laughs, as if at a bawdy joke, then concludes, "We taking garlic, you know. And is putting there, like suppository."

"A clove of garlic?"

"Yes. Is working very good."

She is still coughing. "Go see a doctor," urges Édith. Fadila had told her she has a family doctor where she has been going for years: "Is not expensive."

"But I no have money," she says now, gloomily.

She works roughly twenty-five hours a week, her rent is €120, she's as frugal as they come: she must have enough for a co-payment for a visit to her doctor.

"Don't your children help you?" asks Édith.

Fadila is taken aback: "My children? Is me helping them, is them ask me for money!"

Her daughters and their husbands, her son, all five of them are between forty and fifty years of age and they are all working: whatever next?

"You give money to your children?" echoes Édith.

"Life is expensive," says Fadila.

She explains that her son's wife doesn't work, that she was brought up to have whatever she wants, she buys "chocolate, almonds," their little girl has everything she needs. "When I go see them they asking for money."

Édith suddenly remembers the credit card Fadila uses only at the ATM in Pantin, and the code that her son knows by heart.

"When your son goes with you to withdraw money on your credit card, do you give him that money?"

Fadila shrugs: "'Course."

She doesn't say that her daughters do likewise. And she doesn't even reproach her son for asking for help. She never reproaches him for anything.

Her daughters, on the other hand, neglect her, which she cannot help but point out. They never go to visit her. They don't call often enough. There are even times when they are in the neighborhood and don't even come up to say hello.

She cannot understand this. "If you living not far from your mother, you go seeing her, spend some time with her. If he going shopping you going shopping with her. I'm no young, after all."

A silence. "Aïcha she racist," she says finally.

"Racist?"

"Yes. All she care is friends, I go seeing friends, I sleeping friend's house. And me she say she no have time seeing me. With me is racist."

Édith cannot help but feel irritated when she sees how

Fadila's expectations differ, depending on whether she is speaking of her daughters or her son.

"Your son could look after you a bit more, too, no?"

"No, is daughters," says Fadila again. "Is daughters they gotta look after is mama."

"And sons? Don't they have to look after their mother?"

"No, sons is gotta look after is wife."

She arrives one day with a full page of words copied out the day before—her first and last name clearly written but all run together, and then, similarly: *NASSERLARBIT, AÏCHAREREARERBRERC.*

Édith separates *NASSER, LARBIT, AÏCHA*, drawing circles around each name. Fadila copies them out again flawlessly, making her letters cleanly and quickly. But even immediately afterwards she cannot write them from memory.

Édith gives her a new sheet with models. She insists upon the importance of working on her own at home. "It's what we call homework. Everyone who learns to read and write has to do it, every day, in addition to their class."

"So is going in my head."

"Yes, so it goes in your head."

Fadila is feeling bloated today. It happens on a regular basis, she has bad digestion.

Her daughter Zora comes to do the ironing in her place. A good-looking woman with a smooth face under her white headscarf, calm, reserved.

When Édith gets ready to pay her, she seems offended: "No, no money. I'm doing it for my mother."

Right. Édith will pay Fadila for Zora's hours. She has seen daughters who behave more ungratefully toward their mother.

"Is feeling a little better." Fadila is back at work.

She used the time while she was sick at home to practice writing. "Twice," she says, raising her index and middle fingers on her right hand.

"And what did you write?"

"Nasser, Aïcha, is name my children."

"Well done. Can you write them without a model?"

"No. I doing with paper next to me."

"So your first and last name: you must know them by heart."

But no. Today Fadila can't recall them, no.

Reading is not going all that well, either. Édith points to *MA*, the beginning of *MADAME*, and Fadila reads *Fa. AI*, the beginning of *Aïcha*: Fadila reads *Nasser*. Édith points out the difference in length of the two words, the difference in the initial letters. Clearly the analytical approach isn't working, but neither is the global approach.

When it comes to copying *RUE LABORDE*, Fadila runs the two words together. She has not yet assimilated the notion of a word. Édith shows her that there are medium-sized words, very long words, and little words with two letters, and that you can tell a word precisely because it is separated from the others by a blank space on either side. "Letters are attached, but not words," she says again.

They are interrupted by a telephone call. When Édith returns, Fadila is finishing copying out a word she found on the cover of the magazine *Le Débat* which had been left on the table, the word *CULTURE*. Not a single mistake. Édith congratulates her. Fadila raises an eyebrow: "Is not enough is writing, I gotta know what is mean."

Édith decides to try something more aggressive. She sets her little laptop down between them. On the screen is the first page of the *Alphalire* method.

"It's a game for learning how to read," she says airily, as if she had never brought it up before. "Look—"

Fadila interrupts her. "I no see nothing, is computer."

Édith argues with her. "It's like a sheet of paper, you know. If you can see the letters on a page, you can see them on a computer."

"I no see," insists Fadila. She is determined: "My son say is giving headache."

Fadila studies a photograph that came in the mail for Édith. Two young newlyweds smiling outside a church.

"Is family?" she asks.

"My goddaughter." Édith adds that the young woman is a doctor, her husband is a teacher and they are going to do a year of volunteer service in Africa.

"Is good," says Fadila. "No is many is doing like that."

She knows several young Moroccan men who would like to get married but who cannot find suitable girls. "Today girls they is not serious, is running around, too much boys."

Édith, who knows what these boys would call a suitable girl, protests: "There are a lot of perfectly serious young women."

"No, is finish. You staying here all day long. You no know what is go on."

"But your granddaughters are married," says Édith. "They're fine girls."

Fadila cannot deny it. It is all thanks to their father, she explains, Zora's husband. "Zora her husband he say is anything happen he cutting throat to everyone."

"He wouldn't do that to his own daughters, now would he?"

"Yes, is his daughters, is wife, is everybody. Zora is always afraid. Real Moroccan man he that way."

23

F adila is furious. That very morning, a woman whom she has been working for over the last few months lost her temper with her (over her schedule?) and told her she could replace her with ten other people. With so many people out of work . . .

Édith tries to calm her down: "You should have told her that you can find work in ten other houses."

To no avail. "Is someone working your house is like family," says Fadila. "You no has to say is ten others can replace you."

For her, work creates a reciprocal bond between two people that goes far beyond an employment contract. You don't go undoing those bonds in an offhand, unilateral way. On the contrary, you do everything you can never to break them.

She knows her son's telephone number by heart. Édith tries to persuade her that if she knows it by heart, one number after the other, she will be able to write it.

It's not altogether true, but almost. Where numbers are concerned, the analytical method seems to work. Numbers, of course, are not nearly as abstract as letters, provided you keep to their basic function, and use them essentially for measuring quantities.

Tension is running high this particular Tuesday. Fadila wanted to come to work at the beginning of the afternoon but, when she got there, she realized she had forgotten her key.

There was no one at home. So she had to go back to her house to fetch it then come back.

Now she finds that the shirts hanging to dry have been buttoned from top to bottom, and she has to unbutton them to iron them, and it's exasperating. She comes to complain to Édith, just when Édith is struggling with a particularly tricky passage. "Blame my husband," says Édith, who knows that Fadila respects Gilles and is very fond of him.

She immediately regrets her words, not because she used him to get out of it—she wasn't lying, after all—but for telling Fadila that her husband, in addition to being amiable and cheerful, hangs up the laundry to dry.

Fadila tells Édith how in the métro she found the direction to La Courneuve right away, because she knows the *L*. For the first time she didn't have to ask another passenger to confirm whether she was on the right platform. "Just like everybody," she says.

Édith takes her by the shoulders. "You see! Now you've understood that the first letter of a word can help you to recognize it."

Of her own accord Fadila says she would like to be able to read the names of the directions of the two or three métro lines she tends to use. Édith seizes the opportunity and writes: *LA COURNEUVE* and *VILLEJUIF*.

Fadila may have been discouraged at not being admitted to a literacy course, but she hasn't given up for all that. She wants so badly to be normal (she wants to be able to read like everyone else. Being illiterate is not just a handicap, it's also a source of shame) and she has a great need for autonomy (it's so trying, always having to depend on others). She isn't asking for help or assistance; on the contrary, she would like to have the means to be able to get by on her own.

One day she comes with a form from the Social Security

which she does not know how to fill out. Her family doctor gave it to her already a while ago. It's the form that has to be used to choose one's primary care provider.

The doctor filled in his part of the form. Fadila would like Édith to help her with the rest.

"You can do it," says Édith. "It's not complicated. Here you write your first name, there your last name, and then you sign here."

Fadila is afraid she will "make a mess." Édith shows her that they can avoid the risk by writing in pencil first, and if it's okay, she'll go over it in ink. With no further ado Fadila fills in the blanks for *First Name* and *Last Name.*

Just as she is about to sign she asks, "I do like always at the bank?"

Édith is familiar with her usual zigzag on the back of her checks, and stops her: "No, do it the way the doctor did, look. Here he wrote his name, Marc Aubenton, and here he signed M. AUBENTON. You can sign F. AMRANI."

A printed envelope came with the form. Fadila folds the paper in two and slips it in the envelope. "You gotta stamp?" she says to Édith, "I no having at home."

Her son and daughter-in-law are expecting a second child. Édith congratulates her.

Fadila screws up her face. It's not that her son isn't pleased, he only has one child so far and he has to have a son someday. But it's already a tight squeeze in a studio that measures only 215 square feet. What will it be like with four of them? Nasser asked long ago to be re-housed, to no avail. There is nothing on offer, or nothing acceptable.

"And what about your daughter-in-law," asks Édith, "is she all right? She isn't too tired?"

"She is," says Fadila harshly. "Is sleeping all the time, never going out."

She cannot understand why this young woman who has "everything she needing thank God" coddles herself to such a degree. She certainly wouldn't have spent all day sleeping just because she was pregnant.

24

Fadila would do a better job of reading if she didn't always try too quickly to guess before anything else.

Édith asks her to take one of the envelopes addressed to her out of her bag and read it. It should work: Fadila knows perfectly well what is written on the envelope.

But instead of saying MADAME she says Aïcha. And when she realizes her mistake, and properly identifies MADAME, for the following word she reads AMRANI: it says FADILA, she should have recognized it, there is no word she knows better than that one. And AMRANI comes right after.

Once her memory has been refreshed, she manages better. It is obvious that these work sessions are few and far between.

Édith spends a week in London at a symposium on translation. She is in charge, with a colleague, of the days devoted to literary translation. It has taken a lot of work, but things are going smoothly, their discussions are practical and fruitful. There are a few memorable moments as they debate the sample cases, translating Mia Couto or Cormac McCarthy.

No sooner is she back in Paris than she has to leave again. Her father, who lives alone in Lyon, has to undergo an emergency operation. She stays with him for the forty-eight hours he is at the clinic and the days that follow, the time it takes to organize the home care that he will need for a time.

When Édith next sees Fadila, three weeks have gone by.

There was a post-it on the washing machine, a very recognizable *FADIIA* and two numbers one above the other. Édith gathered that Fadila had written down her hours for each of the two Tuesdays she'd come during her absence, but she was unable to decipher the numbers.

Fadila knows what she wrote, however, she can read her own writing: a *2* for two hours and underneath it a *1* plus a little dash for an additional half hour.

Once she has finished her ironing, she comes to Édith and asks, "You having time today?"

Édith suggests they start with what she knows well, in principle, writing her first and last name and, to Édith's astonishment, Fadila writes both words correctly without hesitating.

It is the first time. Édith is puzzled, but delighted; she hides her bewilderment but not her joy.

"Is writing at home," says Fadila.

"Every day?"

"No!" She rolls her eyes to the ceiling. "Sometimes."

"That explains it," says Édith, who understands even less about the process as time goes by.

Fadila leaves early this Tuesday, she has some cooking to do. It is the Day of Ashura tomorrow. "Is holiday, like Christmas." Special dishes are prepared, "normally is chicken," but not this year. Because of the bird flu epidemic Fadila no longer eats poultry; nor do any of her family. And yet she does like it: "Is prefer chicken to meat." But with everything she's seen on television, "Is disgusting," she says. Her children as well, "They think is disgusting."

Édith repeats what you can read in all the papers, that there is no danger in France, and you can go on safely buying chicken, unlike in Vietnam or Turkey. She reminds Fadila that ten years earlier it was beef you weren't supposed to eat, because of mad cow disease.

Fadila remembers. She chuckles: "Is politics." Or perhaps

she meant politicians, because she goes on to say, "They has to talk, otherwise is television going to close! Has to find something to say, otherwise is no more work!"

She has come early. "I coming early to see Aïcha—is a bitch. Is not there."

Édith points out that she's used a harsh word.

"I doing on purpose," says Fadila. "I stay all weekend at home, no one they calling, no one to see how I doing. You think is normal, old woman all alone and no one they calling? Aïcha she no has a husband."

That's another problem, says Édith. But Fadila goes on to explain, "If she no having husband, she can looking after his mother."

"You could have called your daughters yourself," says Édith.

"No," protests Fadila, "Is me old one, is me the others they gotta call asking news."

Édith recalls a passage in Proust, in *Swann's Way*, where at a reception Madame de Gallardon tries to attract the attention of her young cousin, the Princesse de Guermantes, and when she is unsuccessful, she takes umbrage: *It is not up to me to take the first step, I'm twenty years older than she is.*

"Who I gonna go to when I'm old, retired, huh?" fulminates Fadila. "My daughter is look like I not even her mother. How he going looking after me when I'm old? They no looking after me even when I has good health!"

She does not calm down until it is time to leave. Édith suggests they do a bit of reading, but all she hears in reply is a curt, "'Nother time."

Several times in a row the same thing happens. "Not today, I'm tired," or "I no having time," or "Next time." But she agrees to take some homework with her. She says she will do it.

She brings back a sheet that proves she really has worked at home. She has copied her name and address, and she's in a good mood.

"It's good, there are no mistakes," says Édith, after she's had a look. "But you've written the words any old how, *rue, madame, Paris, 62, Laborde* . . ."

Fadila interrupts: "Is no matter!"

Édith tries to convince her that it does: "Think of the mailman. Poor guy, what's he supposed to do if he sees an address like this on an envelope: 62 Amrani Paris Madame?"

Fadila howls with laughter, something she only does during their lessons.

Édith however worries about these words scattered all over the place. It is this type of incompetence, this lack of an organizing principle within her abstract thoughts that must be preventing Fadila from making any progress. If the word order doesn't matter, there can be no intelligible text, no possible reading.

Easter is coming, the shops are full of chocolates, eggs, fish, bunnies, and bells.

"You no buying chocolate?" asks Fadila.

Édith replies that all this commercial pressure annoys her and that Easter is a religious holiday that has nothing to do with chocolate. Fadila is friendly, attentive, the way she is whenever they touch on spiritual matters.

"I understand," she says. "Is not just eggs, Easter."

The third trimester has started and still no one has called back from the *mairie* of the sixteenth arrondissement. "You mustn't forget to sign up in June," says Édith. "This time for sure there will be a place for you."

25

É dith is away from Paris quite frequently and does not see Fadila for two weeks at a stretch.

When they meet, Fadila immediately says, "I been writing at home." She laughs: "Yesterday I doing a lot. I thinking, you coming back, has to do lesson, has to work."

The words she has written are all run together, sometimes swallowing each other (*FADILMRANI*). Not a single one is as it should be (*NSSER, MADZAE, RUELABDE.*)

She is in a mood. "Is something wrong?" asks Édith.

She shakes her head and turns on her heels. But five minutes later she comes back: "You wanna know what is wrong? Is always something wrong with children."

Aïcha, again. She hasn't called her mother for three weeks. Perhaps she has her own problems, suggests Édith.

"No. Is just like that, Aïcha, she cutting off everything, dunno why. Just when she getting married . . ."

"Her daughter is getting married?"

"No, is Aïcha!" moans Fadila. "She is old, is fifty years, is getting married one young guy."

A thirty-year-old undocumented Moroccan: it is obvious to Fadila and her whole family that the fellow is getting married merely in order to have his status regularized.

Aïcha's grown children are furious. Fadila lectures her daughter: why does she need a man in the house? This one has no job, he'll cost her a fortune. Already Aïcha complains she cannot call her mother "because she no having money." And when the fellow has taken her for all she's worth then finds some work, he'll vanish.

Yet Aïcha does know what a husband is, she had one, a drinker, violent, good for nothing; he died from liver cancer. But she won't listen. When her mother speaks to her she looks at the ground and doesn't answer. What can anyone do to stop someone this age heading straight for disaster?

"Is daytime I working," says Fadila, "but at night I no sleeping, I seeing things, I seeing everything is gonna happen."

She's in a hurry, she has to go to Boulogne to a halal butcher for the cow's feet with chickpeas they cook in Morocco. They'll do their reading another day.

She calls to cancel—for once ahead of time; she can't come this Tuesday afternoon but she'll make up for it tomorrow morning, Wednesday.

Édith needs to be alone in the morning. That is when she does her best work. She tells Fadila that the change of schedule does not work for her.

"I no see why not," says Fadila harshly.

Édith doesn't insist. In Fadila's place, she wouldn't see why not either.

Her son's child has been born, a second daughter. "Is fine baby," she says, without another word.

Probably she was not allowed to get involved at the time of the birth. Her son has taken yet another step away from his mother and closer to his wife. Once again, Fadila is suffering from the fact that she does not have the position that should be hers at her age—the position that would have been hers had she had a normal life in Morocco.

She emerges from her silence to say, tersely, "After you having children, life is fucked."

Bitter. Stoic. Torn. Brutal. Not about to be contradicted.

She has some time today. She wants to try and write, but she has nothing left "in her head," as she puts it.

Édith has her copy her name and address from an envelope. She does it without error. She remembers to separate the words with a blank space, and even points it out.

But when Édith shows her the *MADAME* she forgot to copy in front of her first name and asks her which word it is, she says, "Nasser."

"Have a good look." Édith is within an inch of giving up. "*M* and *N* are different, they sound different, they're written differently."

And she writes out a card to illustrate the principle: every word has an initial letter,

   M for *MADAME*
   N for *NASSER*
   F for *FADILA*, and so on.

Fadila takes the card and gets to her feet, she's got it, she'll "go over at home."

But how long will she spend? How many times will she work on it? Édith follows her with her gaze. Half an hour would be a minimum, half an hour every day. How can you ask that of a woman who is weary and disgusted and who sees herself as an old woman? A woman who has lost her roots, who sits alone at night in a tiny room, who cannot switch off the television for fear of being devoured by her anguish.

"You see?" she asks, laughing. "Diana: is old one she put Koran on her head."

"The Koran?"

"Yes. Is one lady she giving me book, is putting Koran on her head. Is queen she no want but he is winning."

"Ah, you mean Camilla!"

"Yes, she getting married, has Koran on her head."

"The crown."

"Yes, she is winning and the other one, poor thing, the pretty one, is dead."

26

Of her own accord Fadila reminds Édith of the literacy course at the *mairie* of the sixteenth arrondissement. "Has to signing up."

She'll go on her own. She knows the way, it's only a short distance from the rue de la Pompe where she goes to the family doctor she likes.

The enrolment cost her fifty euros. "It's not expensive," says Édith, "when you think, for three two-hour classes per week for a whole year."

"I know," she says. "Fifty euros is insurance. Only insurance."

Fadila has been hesitating for a while now, but this time she's made up her mind, she is going to drop one of her employers. This is the first time she has mentioned this man to Édith. It's obvious he's been taking her for a ride. He has always told her that he would enroll her for benefits "with is government pay slip," but he's done no such thing. He tells her he's going away, on a trip, and asks her not to come for a few weeks, then he calls and says he needs her urgently. His apartment is utterly filthy. She doesn't believe this travel business. In her opinion, the man never leaves Paris, he just waits until the filth gets unbearable to call Fadila.

And this morning when she was working there she was told not to make any noise, no running the vacuum cleaner, because "is his friend sleeping in the bedroom."

"This is man he going with men, is too bad," she says. "I meeting his mother, he's been study, is smart guy. Is pity when people they go ruining life like that. Is no children, is no family, it breaks your heart."

There are days when things suddenly click into place, and her progress seems to have moved forward a notch.

Édith tries once again to get the principle of the Meccano across, deconstructing words into letters. On one side she has the word *FADILA*, and on the other, in the textbook, the column of the twenty-six letters in the alphabet. She points to the *F* in the word and asks Fadila to find it in the list. Fadila can't see it.

"The *F*, you know it. Look, let me write it for you."

No response.

Édith goes through the alphabet one letter after the other, and with each letter she asks, "Is this one the *F*?"

At the *A*, Fadila says, "This one is RER," and at the *B* and *C*, too.

She recognizes the *F* when Édith comes to it.

She manages to find the second letter of her first name, the *A* they just mentioned, at the head of the list.

For the *D*, she comes right out and says she won't find it. "We saw it just a minute ago," insists Édith, and she manages to locate it.

For the *I*, which to Édith seems so easy to identify, Fadila initially says she doesn't see it, but then puts her finger on it.

As for the last letter of her first name, she knows it's the *A* at the beginning of the alphabet, she no longer hesitates.

She is relaxed. Édith tells her again that once she knows the twenty-six letters, she'll know how to read. She shrugs, discreetly, like someone who doesn't really believe it.

Fadila is in tears. She is due to go to Morocco at the end of

July, one month from now, and for the first time she has allowed herself be talked into taking the plane, but now she's just found out that all her children and grandchildren are leaving before her. She was supposed to travel with Nasser, but he's changed his ticket, along with his wife's and daughters'. He found a much cheaper flight, but he's leaving a week before his mother. Zora and her family are leaving two weeks earlier by car. And Aïcha? She and Fadila aren't on speaking terms.

If she were going to do the trip all alone by bus, she wouldn't worry. She's used to it. But she's never taken the plane. She's occasionally been to an airport, and she always feels completely lost in a place like that. She won't be able to manage on her own. And now this ticket, which one of her grandsons reserved for her on the internet, has cost her three hundred euros and it can't be reimbursed.

Last night at Zora's she lost her temper. Her son-in-law Mohammed was insulting, the way he talked back to her. He's a brute, she doesn't want to see him anymore. He drinks. He tells lies. "One day he tell Zora is one his friend he sleep with her!"

"Have they been married for long?"

"Is thirty years! Problem is, Zora she in loving with him! She putting up with him! He going after other women, is always doing like that. Already in Morocco is never eating with is wife and children. He coming home late, he wearing nice suit, is perfume, is going out until five o'clock in the morning.

"I telling Zora: What is going on? You ironing his shirt one o'clock in the morning, he going with women you no say nothing? She rather say nothing, have peace and quiet. Never I accepting like that."

"Does he have a profession?"

"Yes, is working electrician."

"And if he drinks, doesn't he have problems at work?"

"No. Is working, is drinking, is working, is drinking."

"Well, so much the better, I suppose. It wouldn't help matters if he were to lose his job."

"I no caring if he have accident. I sorry to say that, but is no good life for Zora. Drunk, drunk, always drunk!

"One day, I been Zora's house, is going with Nasser. Is Mohammed he say, Nasser, come on, we going out. Nasser asking me lend him 50 euros. Zora is no worry, she going sleeping. I no can sleep, is hurting (she points to her stomach), is heart beating (her breast), I walking walking in the house, I waiting. At two o'clock I waking up big son Younes, I tell him he get dressed. He coming with me to bar in the street. Is boss he close at ten o'clock but after is keeping customers inside, everyone they drinking, is music, with Younes we listening, can hear the music: that is where they is. At four o'clock is coming back, Mohammed. I telling him off good and proper! I say, Where is Nasser? He say, I take him home to sleep. I been so mad I go crazy. I no speaking him and Zora for two months."

27

The French football team have won the World Cup semi-final. The final match will be held on Sunday.

"So, is bravo for the French!" says Fadila the moment she walks in the door.

"Did you watch the match on television?"

"No. I no watching 'cause I getting mad if the French they no win."

"You're for the French team?"

"What you expect! Is eating piece of bread!"

"What do you mean?"

"We is in France, we eat in France, is want France to win. France she doing a lot for poor people. Is giving welfare to people he has no work, is school cost nothing, is the social security . . . Is why God he always giving rain, flowers, trees, all that. God is watching, is what we believing."

"So France team she losing."

She has taken the matter to heart, it would seem.

"Yes. It doesn't matter."

"No. Is no worth is getting annoyed about it." Firmly: "Is a game."

The latest news is that one of her granddaughters might be able to go with her to the airport at the end of July—Khadija, who is a hairdresser at a big beauty salon on the Champs-Elysées. But it has not been finalized, and Fadila is beginning to get impatient. No matter how often she leaves messages on her granddaughter's cell phone, her calls have never been returned.

"I no care," she says, "I going to Champs-Elysées is talking with her. She no wanting I go Champs-Elysées with headscarf, I no care."

"Why can't you go to the Champs-Elysées wearing a headscarf?" says Édith, astonished.

Fadila laughs and raises her chin. "She no want 'cause she is chic!"

Before leaving Fadila asks, not to read for a while—she doesn't have time—but for some homework. Édith ruffles through the little pile of papers that have served in the past as material for their lessons. "Here," she says, taking out one of the sheets, "your children's first names."

For some reason she cannot recall, *NASSER* has been written four times on the sheets, on four successive lines.

Fadila takes the sheet, looks at it and, instead of leaving, she sits down. Édith points to *AÏCHA*: Fadila reads *Nasser*.

"No, look." Édith points to the first *NASSER*: "Here he is, Nasser."

Then she slides her finger down to the second *NASSER*, on the line below. Fadila reads *Zora*.

"Are you sure?" says Édith.

Fadila blurts, "Aïcha! Zora! Larbit!"

Édith stops her, asks her to look carefully at the two *NASSER*s written one on top of the other on the first two lines. Fadila realizes they are identical.

Édith shows her the third and fourth *NASSER* underneath. Fadila takes a while to grasp that this is the same word once again, and again.

She is beside herself. Her granddaughter Khadija has gone

on vacation, just when Fadila was counting on her to take her to the airport the following week.

As for Zora, she has already left, too, by car with her family as planned, but did she say goodbye to her mother?

"Bitch!" says Fadila, spitting out the word. "You say goodbye when you is going away! You no knowing what can happen, maybe is dying. You say goodbye."

She stabs at a tear. "I no having luck my children. My son I no asking nothing, he has wife is not my daughter, I leave them alone. Girls is not the same. In Morocco is girls they gotta do everything for his mother."

And Aïcha, whom she never mentions anymore? "Did she get married?" asks Édith. "Did she marry that young man?"

Fadila gives her a fierce look. "I dunno. Aïcha I no seeing."

And immediately afterwards, in the same tone: "No, she no getting married. But is crazy anyway!"

On July 26, when Fadila is due to leave, Édith will be in Geneva. But Gilles will find a way to take Fadila to Charles de Gaulle airport. Departure is scheduled for late afternoon, he'll be able to get off in time.

On the appointed day, at the end of the morning, he gets a call from Fadila. She is not taking the plane after all. They never brought her her ticket. The grandson who made the reservation has left Paris. Her daughters are in Morocco. She's out three hundred euros.

She has just made an arrangement with "is one man Aïcha she know" who will give her a lift in his car. She will be leaving in two days' time. And of course she will have to pay for this trip by car.

28

When Édith next sees Fadila, in early September, she finds her pale with rage. "I so mad," she says, over and over. She did not particularly want to see any of her family in Morocco, but none of them tried to see her, either, not one of them got in touch with her, and she has not gotten her money back.

It is out of the question for her to call anybody. If anything, they should be calling her, she says repeatedly.

"It's true," concedes Édith, "you do have the right to an explanation."

"I no care nothing about explanation."

She wants to get her three hundred euros back, period. As for Zora and her family, it's all over between them.

She asks Édith to write to Zora for her. "I'll do it," says Édith, "but you have to dictate the letter."

Fadila is not at a loss for words. "Your mom she asking you give back three hundred euros," she dictates. "You is bringing in envelope her house where she living."

So who did she stay with in Morocco, since she was not with any of her family?

"Well, is my house!" she says.

She did not want to risk running into any of her children, so she didn't go to Casablanca, or Rabat, or Agadir, where they might have met; she left right away for her village "in mountain is not far Essaouira."

There in "is big house," which she insists belongs to her, or at least half of it, she made the acquaintance of her brother, the half-brother she had never seen. He is married to a "very nice" woman, they have four "very nice" children. "Is calling me auntie, is wanting me stay there. They is crying and crying when I going."

She is determined to stay in touch. The family's poverty distresses her. The children are ragged, they have none of the things her grandchildren in France have. She is going to send them clothes and money.

On her way out she comes of her own accord to sit next to Édith.

"I forgetting everything," she says.

"You didn't practice at all?"

"I doing nothing at all!"

You don't forget things like this, Édith assures her. They'll start again. It will come back.

"Has to!" says Fadila, who hasn't forgotten that the class at the *mairie* of the sixteenth arrondissement will be starting on September 25th.

"Off we go, then."

"Slow-slow."

They start over, first name, last name, address. Fadila can still write her first name from memory, but not her last name. She copies out her address, more or less without any mistakes.

"And how is your daughter-in-law? The baby?" asks Édith, who would like to know if Fadila is seeing her beloved son, at least.

"Is okay," says Fadila. "Poor woman, she is getting presents but no one they giving her brand names!"

So Fadila, the grandmother, went to Jacadi and bought two pairs of pajamas for her three-month-old granddaughter.

As she walks past the sofa Fadila stops: there are always some recent newspapers lying on it, and now she picks one up. She holds it in both hands and stares at it intensely.

"Have you seen something that interests you?"

"What is this?" she asks.

This, on the cover of the television section of *Le Monde*, is a photograph of youths from the *banlieues* throwing stones at shop windows.

"They've made a documentary about the young people in the *banlieues*," says Édith. "That business in Clichy-sous-Bois, you remember?"

"I has to watch. Is already finish?"

Édith checks.

"No, it's on tonight. See, Tuesday the nineteenth, that's today."

"Show me," says Fadila.

She examines the line Édith is pointing to, the date and the day, at the top of the page.

"Is numbers is okay. What I don' know, is Tuesday, Monday, Thursday . . ."

"The days? Well, we can learn them," says Édith.

While Fadila watches she writes *MARDI 19* on a sheet of paper.

"Is look like *LARBIT*," says Fadila.

"Well done, that's right. But there are some differences, look."

Édith writes *LARBIT* just above *MARDI* so that the two *A*'s are on top of each other, and the two *R*'s as well.

"You see," she says, "in *MARDI* and in *LARBIT*"—she stresses the *ar* orally, and circles the two *AR*'s with a pencil—there are two letters that are exactly the same. Not the others . . ."

She writes *MAR* across from *MARDI*, and beneath it she writes *LAR* across from *LARBIT*.

"What is saying, there?" asks Fadila, pointing to *MAR*.

Fadila can decipher neither *MAR* nor *LAR*.

She still cannot read syllables on their own. She can sometimes make out the elements that are shared by two words, but if the words are deconstructed she can no longer recognize the very same elements.

In a few days, on Monday the 25th, classes will begin at the *mairie* of the sixteenth arrondissement. Fadila will go on her own, she knows where it is.

"Does that work for you, six thirty?" asks Édith. "It's not too early? Will you have finished work?"

Fadila doesn't foresee any problems.

"I figure out."

In fact, something else is troubling Édith. She remembers how she had started off teaching cursive handwriting to Fadila, and that it had turned out to be very difficult for her, so they had gone on to block capitals, which were easier for her. And Édith is afraid that at the literacy class they will start off using cursive.

"Do you remember that there are two ways of writing?" she asks Fadila.

She shows her in the textbook words in cursive and others in capital letters, and reminds Fadila that she is acquainted with the two sorts of writing.

"How did your first class go?"

Fadila says calmly, "Is going fine."

They are a big group but the classroom is huge, there were at least twenty tables in there. A "very nice" lady divided up the students. "I sitting at table with Moroccans." In this subgroup there is a woman who is most definitely older than Fadila and who has also never been to school.

She has brought with her, to show Édith, the workbook

that was handed out to all the students, to show Édith. On page 2, neatly written, every letter on its line, are the twenty-six letters of the alphabet, in cursive handwriting.

Fadila doesn't point it out. Édith also thinks it's better not to say anything at this stage.

The nice lady has asked them to copy out these twenty-six letters for the following class. Not for one moment does Fadila entertain the idea of doing it on her own. She has made an appointment with her Tunisian neighbor on the landing, who has agreed to help her between classes. They will be meeting this evening.

This is the first time she has mentioned any such outside help to Édith.

"Is your neighbor with you at the class?"

Not at all, says Fadila. The neighbor has been reading and writing since she was a child. She's in her forties. They get along, the two of them, and help each other out from time to time. They celebrated the beginning of Ramadan together a few days ago.

Édith wonders if this could be a way for Fadila to try another learning method, and to change her tutor at the same time as she changes her method, for Édith herself to put an end once and for all to the disappointing effort of the last year and a half.

29

The following week everything is all messed up. "Is finish, I no going back," says Fadila. "I walk out the class!"

She is so furious she can hardly speak. Édith takes a while to piece together what happened.

At the second class, their teacher was no longer the nice lady from the first time, but a young woman, "is very nervous," and Fadila knew why: she was a heavy smoker, and because they were not allowed to smoke in the classroom she was sucking on one lozenge after the other.

The break came right at the beginning of the class. It didn't take long.

To copy out her letters, Fadila asked for her neighbor's help as agreed. She shows her workbook to Édith: the first ten letters look like models, each one neatly on its line. It is obvious that the following lines were not written by the same hand: Fadila had taken over and, visibly, was writing on her own. The result is a pattern of irregular graffiti that is hard to recognize as letters of the alphabet.

The lady teacher walked behind the students to check their workbooks. When she saw Fadila's, she got angry: "You didn't do this," she said, pointing to the first ten lines.

Fadila laughed: "'Course not! I no know how to writing, I not writing that."

Once she had completed her tour, the teacher, still very nervous, went up to the blackboard. In very large letters, with chalk, she wrote the day of the week, the date and the month, and asked everyone to copy it at the top of page 3 in their workbook.

This time it was Fadila who lost her temper: "I not knowing how to write, how you want me is writing that?"

"You copy it!" insisted the teacher.

So Fadila stood up, gathered up her things, said goodbye and left the room.

Édith calls the person in charge at the center, the woman she had spoken to several times on the phone the previous year. An intelligent woman, who agrees that it was a false start, and she would like Fadila to come back. In the course of the conversation she corrects Édith: one should no longer say illiterate, but unschooled, and she insists the students have not been grouped by nationality; they are divided up according to their level.

Fadila won't hear of going back. "I no wasting time with is business," she says, more than once.

It is the third week of Ramadan, she is exhausted. She has new things to worry about. She has just found out that she has to vacate her room before the end of the year. The woman who had been renting her the room without ever giving her a receipt is moving out.

"Is she selling it?" asks Édith.

"'Course not, is no hers, the apartment!"

It all adds up. This tenant was subletting the maid's room of her apartment. Illegally. Fadila came across a housing certificate that the woman had finally agreed to give her, in the event she might need it for administrative purposes: on the certificate it states that she is being housed for free, anyway that is what her daughter-in-law read to her. Therefore she has no basis on which to stay there. She is obliged to leave.

"Hold on a minute," says Édith, who would be surprised if

they could throw out into the street a woman in her situation who had in fact been renting her room for years.

They go together to the office of social services near the rue de Laborde. A social worker confirms to Fadila that she does have rights, in spite of everything, and she advises her, if one day she finds her door locked and her belongings on the landing, to go immediately to the police. At the same time she has her fill out a housing application, but warns her that she could wait years for subsidized housing in Paris. The best thing would be to start looking on the housing market without delay.

By the time they are back outside, night has fallen. They go a few hundred yards down the street together. At the first intersection, Édith stops. "I'll leave you here," she says, waving in the direction of the Place Saint-Augustin, "I'm going to take the métro over there."

"No, no taking métro," says Fadila urgently. "Is night. You has to take taxi. I giving money for taxi."

Édith thanks her, declines, but wonders if once again she has not made a faux pas.

One evening there is a knock on Fadila's door. Two gentlemen she does not know introduce themselves: the owner of the room and his son. She has to leave, says the owner. Next month there will be a new tenant in the apartment, and they will need the room.

Fadila is losing sleep over it. No matter how often Édith tells her they cannot evict her by force, she wants to move out. But she doesn't know where to go. Her children have no room for her. No one will help her. All anyone says, when she tells them about it, is not to budge, wait to be evicted, because the only way to get the social services to house you is to be out on the street.

In fact, her son has not sat around doing nothing. He has an idea. He suggests she come to Pantin, not far from his place. The town has a hostel for foreign workers, where mainly North Africans live, and she could get a spot there.

Fadila absolutely refuses to live there. It's a mixed hostel, with two floors for men and one for women. "Is people saying women in the hostel they go seeing the men. Maybe I old, but is old women saying they find women for the men. I no want nothing to do with that."

Still, she goes to fill out an application. She cannot say no to her son. And besides, you never know, if things get bad at the rue de Laborde, the hostel might be an interim solution.

In fact, she has her own plan. She is "fed up with everything." She wants to go back to Morocco. This summer her half-brother suggested she come and live with his family in their father's house in the village.

"Would you get along with his wife?"

No problem. She's a young woman, and "very nice." And the children are "very nice." When Fadila left at the end of August, they were clinging to her and crying. Something that had never happened to her before, Édith gathers.

30

T here have been violent confrontations in Morocco recently, on the border with the Spanish enclaves. Sub-Saharan Africans have massed there in the thousands and forced their way through the barbed wire fences. Moroccan and Spanish police retaliated. People were injured and killed. A few hundred "lucky ones" managed to slip through. There are pages and pages about it in the press.

Édith is reading an article about the situation. No doubt because she can see she is focused on something, Fadila asks, "Is something going on?"

"Yes, in Morocco. Look. Had you heard?"

A photograph shows a young black man with a ladder placed against a fence. Fadila knows all about it: "I seeing all the time on television is Morocco." She cannot contain her rage: what are those foreigners doing there? They have to go home. And so on.

Édith ventures, "Home for them, is extreme poverty."

How could she say such a thing! Fadila sees red.

"Is not poverty! Everyone he is eating, now. Is people they never happy. They not knowing what is poverty."

She knew what poverty was, when she was a child. "One day is someone he feeling too much hot, next day is dead." She recalls a cholera epidemic: "Half of people is dead." That was the way things were. You ate tomatoes and bread and you didn't complain.

"Poverty! If that is poverty, then is poverty everywhere!

Here too is poverty, is no work, social security he no have money . . ."

She fusses: "And they having lots the children! They no have to go having so many the children. Is pills, after all!"

"You see?" she says. "Four airplanes is full the people they sending home."

"I saw," says Édith.

They read, too, that the Moroccan authorities had transported entire busloads of people all the way to the Algerian border, for that is where they had come in, and they abandoned them there in the middle of the desert.

"Is having to go home," concludes Fadila.

Édith doesn't take it any further. She just says the same thing that all the experts on emigration have predicted: these young sub-Saharan Africans will be back. They will try again.

"No," interrupts Fadila. "Is finish. Is no possible no more."

Édith is having trouble concentrating on her work, it's taking her forever. Her father is not well. He cannot stay on his own. She's worked it out with her sisters, she'll spend forty-eight hours every week in Lyon, from Friday morning through Saturday night. And Gilles has just found out that his company will be making cutbacks among the staff. It's not the first time. He might be on the list this time.

"Are you all right?" asks Fadila when she comes in.

Édith has always said, "Fine," but this time she can't help herself: "I'm tired."

Fadila literally laughs in her face, her fist on her hip: "If you saying you tired, what I gonna say, huh? With everything is happening right now?"

At least she has patched things up with her daughter Aïcha. She had a dream, she says. A man was speaking to her on behalf of her mother, her mother who died long ago and whom she loved so dearly. "She is fed up," said the man in the dream. He repeated this several times and Fadila understood that he was talking about her feud with Aïcha. Through him, her mother was telling Fadila that it was time for her to make up with Aïcha.

So sure enough, three days later, last Sunday, Aïcha came to visit, with one of her daughters.

Once, only once, did Édith venture to say, "Maybe it would be a good idea to go back to the class at the *mairie* of the sixteenth arrondissement."

Fadila brushes her suggestion aside: "You think I being in the mood for that?" It's no, once and for all. Even under better circumstances, she would not go back there. "Is woman she making class is crazy."

"Well then you could at least ask to be reimbursed."

"I no caring about the money," says Fadila.

Édith, however, puts in a request for her. At the center, Édith's contact is conciliatory. She doesn't insist on trying to get Fadila to come back. They will send a check to Madame Amrani.

Édith tells Fadila what she has done. Then adds (she feels obliged to at least try): "We can go back to working the two of us."

She is instantly sorry she said anything. It would have been smarter to wait, and let the interested party say whether she wanted to start up again or not.

But Fadila is already saying, curtly, "I giving twenty-five euros my neighbor, she is teaching me."

"And do you have any news of Zora?" asks Édith.

Fadila explodes: "No. I no seeing her anymore, is long time. Is not my daughter. I don't know is name of her children."

Zora has not been in touch since June. "After all," says Fadila, "I being her mother. She maybe just call say hello, how are you? Why she wearing headscarf if she has no heart?"

In all honesty, she knows very well why her daughter doesn't call. "She no want speak to me because I telling her is husband he no have respect, she should no putting up with it. She no like. I say, You kissing his feet, nobody they doing that here, why you doing that? Here is land of freedom! I telling Zora I no want to see him until day I die. He say he earning millions and all day long she going make cleaning people's house. And at night she ironing and cooking for him. She making dinner and she say, What time you want to eat, Mohammed? I telling her, you no say that. She always do that. Already in Morocco she let him walk all over. In Morocco, is maybe, but here, no! In France you no do that."

Édith has not forgotten that at the age of sixteen or seventeen Zora discovered she had two fathers and two mothers—and under what circumstances. "Who chose this husband for her?" she asks.

"Is choosing all alone. I say nothing. Woman has no husband she no can say nothing.

"If Mohammed he earning millions, if he so rich, why his wife not stay home?" she continues. "And he say to Nasser, too: I gonna buy SUV, and is children all have they own car. Why he say that to Nasser? Nasser he no earning very much, he no have car, is no matter, he stay in his place. Why is Mohammed he say, I earning millions? You know what I telling Nasser? I say, is everybody buying SUV, even dog is having SUV!"

In other words: to humiliate Zora, his wife, is one thing. But to humiliate her son Nasser, that's unforgivable.

31

The landlord came and knocked at her door one evening. Fadila told him she would soon be going back to Morocco.

"Before you leave," says Édith worriedly, "you have to ask about your retirement."

Fadila knows. Her daughter-in-law has expressed her concern about it, too.

She goes to see a social worker, who does some rapid calculations and warns her: her retirement pay will be very limited, it is in her interest to go on working as long as possible.

Every month Fadila sends a bundle of clothing to her brother in the village, for his four children. The clothing doesn't cost her anything, people give it to her. "In France is people have plenty, is crazy." But the shipping, through a private carrier, is very costly.

There is a smell of onions in the apartment. Édith is making a potato dish for supper. Fadila, who has only just walked in, lifts the lid: "Is no tomatoes?"

"Tomatoes? No, it's a dish of potatoes and onions, that's all."

In Morocco, Fadila explains, they have tomatoes with everything: lentils, zucchini, turnips, meat and fish, everything. Always onions, always tomatoes.

This reminds Édith of an article she read recently. In Baghdad, the civil servants who were once devoted to Saddam and now proclaim their willingness to serve the elected government are called "tomato-civil servants"—because they go with everything.

"And have you noticed that tomatoes nowadays have no taste at all, they're worthless," says Édith.

Fadila agrees on that score, the tomatoes you find in Paris in December are useless. She can see why Édith doesn't buy any. "But we has to," she says.

She leaves early. She has to go to Pantin to see her son so that he can help her cash the checks that came last week, at the end of November. Lately the bank has refused to let her bring her checks to the teller the way she always has: now she has to fill out a form first. They very kindly handed her a pile of these forms, twenty or more.

"What louts, they could have filled them out for you," says Édith, irritated. "They know very well that you can't do it on your own. If you like, we can do the paperwork together, you and I. It would be a way of working on your numbers and letters."

Fadila declines her offer: "I doing with Nasser."

"It's not a very good idea to carry the checks around with you on the bus." It is not just to trick her that Édith points out the risk: "They could get stolen."

"No," says Fadila peremptorily.

She shows Édith how she puts her handbag inside her big shopping bag, as if this were a form of protection, and she says, "If a person no eat other people's money they no stealing from him neither."

For the pleasure of hearing her repeat what sounds almost like a proverb, Édith asks her again what she said. She explains: "I never taking nobody's money. Is nobody they no do bad, is God protecting them."

As for Zora, according to the same logic, she predicts: "I don' care. She gonna suffer the same from his daughters. What you doing your parents, is your children doing to you."

Édith finds it hard to understand why she is so angry with this daughter whose married life, as Fadila knows only too well, is hell on earth. Yet that is just how things are. Fadila feels humiliated by the fact that her daughter seems to accept her fate. Every week she brings it up. "Has to stop her husband drinking. In the evening he putting car in the garage is going to café right away, is coming home ten-eleven clock, is drunk. She has to make scandal, she say I no sleeping with you no more. I sorry to speak like that. She hiding her hair with her headscarf but under is hair all white. She no using dye. She has to fix hisself up a little! She say is okay but she no happy. Is like a slave. She doesn' do nothing! Her husband he no do nothing in the house. Nowadays is everyone he working in the house. Is director he working in the house. Nasser he coming home he putting pajamas on the kids, after he start setting the table. Is Mohammed he no do nothing!"

It all ties in. Fadila finds fault with her daughter not only for not listening to her, but also for lacking in dignity, for not look-ing after herself, and for putting up uncomplainingly with a husband who's a macho brute.

Her anger also stems from the fact that Zora lives with a man who constantly offends his mother-in-law by humiliating her son. "Is bragging, Mohammed! He always saying all the time is every one his children they having house, every one is having car. If you see how he bragging with me!"

"Have you seen him again? Do you see them, Zora and him?"

"No, I no seeing but is Nasser he tell me. His wife too is tell me. Is Mohammed he no stop bothering Nasser, Come on, we going out tonight . . . But Nasser's wife she no want."

In the end Fadila has decided to move into the hostel in Pantin. It is a week before Christmas. The landlord had said end of the year. He has come knocking on her door several times. Fadila doesn't open anymore, but he shouts through the door that he knows she's there, and then she can't sleep a wink. She'd rather move out.

Not long ago they confirmed a place for her at the hostel: she immediately found a way around her own reservations and said she would take it. She'll be able to move in a few weeks from now, the time it takes for them to give the walls a fresh coat of paint.

She didn't find anything on the market. True, she did not go about it the way Édith would have. For Fadila, house-hunting means asking her family whether anyone has heard of anything to rent. If I were alone in Rabat, thinks Édith, I would do the same.

Fadila has no plans for Christmas. Her children are not on the best of terms these days, so they haven't arranged anything. "Is always one is mad with the others. They live close, is Christmas and they no see each other, you think is normal? They no seeing each other, is holiday for end of Ramadan, they no see each other is Christmas day. Yesterday I crying and crying."

Édith takes her hand: "You will go and spend Christmas day with your son, won't you?"

Fadila doesn't really reply: "My son his sister she not even go seeing baby. He not even calling."

Does she mean Aïcha or Zora? She adds: "When is problems with family is really really bad. Because is people outside you can close the door, but with family you no can close the door."

Édith makes out the check for the month of December. She also fills out the form to send in to the domestic help taxation administration. When Fadila picks up the check, she looks at it and says, "What is check is nothing written there?"

Édith has forgotten to fill in the line where one is meant to spell out the amount.

"Is thanks to you I seeing," says Fadila. "Before I taking to bank I no seeing."

And, of her own accord: "We is having to start again after I moving."

When Édith immediately suggests she write her name on the back of the check, Fadila smiles as if she was expecting this. She writes *FADILA* without difficulty. As for *AMRANI*, she's forgotten how.

She's been with Aïcha to visit her future studio at the hostel in Pantin. It's all right. It's really not far from Nasser's place.

32

Z ora's husband has been beating her. She has a black eye, bruises all over her body, and a constant headache. Fadila relates this to Édith with a heavy heart; she heard it from her son. But it's not enough to make her go and see her daughter. She has told her a hundred times to leave the man and press charges.

"I say: I been crying before you, and I get outta there!" She's fed up that no one listens to her. She shrugs: "Zora she no going police, she no going doctor, nothing. Is thirty years she no do nothing. In Morocco she having like that ten stitch in her head, she no do nothing. What they say, here in France? Love is blind, huh?"

Scornfully, her voice heavy with reproof, she says, "Look at that! Zora she *loving* his husband! She say she wanna die before him. Some people is loving so much . . ."

She thinks it is shameful that her daughter just puts up with the beatings and doesn't react. She feels shame in her place. Twice—she raises two fingers close together—she left a man because he was beating her.

"Was it the best solution?" asks Édith, who thought Fadila had said her first husband wasn't so bad after all, and that she had a soft spot for the third one.

"'Course! I no loving him. I no loving no one, never! I never felt no love for any man!"

She says it forcefully, with satisfaction, the way you might say, I'm not stupid! Let other people get on with such idiotic nonsense.

*

L'Abbé Pierre has died. The news talks of little else, and everyone is upset. "I crying," says Fadila. "That is beautiful life. God he bless him. I think, once a person is nice, God no let him down."

Fadila comes in and finds Édith in the kitchen, standing at the counter eating bread and cheese. It is nearly three o'clock.

"Excuse me, this is my lunch," says Édith. "I'm not exactly running on time."

"You no sitting?" scolds Fadila. "You gotta stop for eating. For vacation and for eating you gotta take time. Otherwise is work, and work is never end."

That idiot Zora still hasn't called her mother. "He knowing what I gonna say, is why."

"She must be scared to death, every night with that brute. Are there children in the house at least?"

Fadila sits up, furious.

"What she afraid of? You no has to be afraid nothing! You no afraid people, is afraid God, is all! If God he no decide is people they kill you, then people no kill you."

"But you can be afraid of being beaten, don't you think?"

Fadila stands like a boxer, her fists raised: "If I was her, I the one do the beating."

Then, inversely, she rounds her back: "Zora is like this! If always she gonna be like this, is everyone they step on her. Her brother he say other day she come his house she eating all her plate then falling asleep. All he do is eating and sleeping."

Fadila shakes her head, dismayed: "I never seen love like that."

That weekend she moved. Her son borrowed a van to transport all the furniture and heavy objects. Her daughter Aïcha went with her by taxi, after filling the trunk with her clothing and odds and ends, in bags.

At rue de Laborde they said a proper goodbye among neighbors. They promised to meet again.

Fadila is in good spirits. She has a real studio, with a window overlooking a garden and, for the first time (in her life, Édith supposes), she has her own bathroom. On every floor in the hostel there is a large common kitchen at the disposal of the residents, and everyone has their own food locker with a key.

"You'll make new friends there," says Édith.

"No." Fadila is categorical. "I no see nobody. Is Arabs, I know, is nothing but problems."

"Even the women?"

"Arab women, you no know them, is blah-blah-blah, she do this, she say that, is nothing but trouble. I no want to see. Anyway I no have time, I leave, I work, I going home, I take shower, making prayer, and sleep."

She seems to be limping slightly.

"You're limping," says Édith. "Did you hurt yourself?"

"Is leg hurting. I try too hard. I going up the stairs, down the stairs, climb on stool, climb off stool."

"Try to get some rest, now."

"Rest? I no have time. No, is leg I don't bother with it, is all. I'm no twenty years old, right? Just I have courage, is all."

She is enjoying the luminosity and tranquillity of her new accommodation. The room is sunny. There is no noise at night. "Is quiet, is clean. On my floor is only three people, is two old women they retired, and me. I no see nobody, is better that way."

The presidential election campaign is in full swing. The confrontation between Ségolène Royal and Nicolas Sarkozy is on everyone's minds.

"He is a man. Is better man is president," decides Fadila.

That is just what a woman who has been crushed by machismo since birth would say, thinks Édith. But how many "born and bred" French people also share her opinion?

33

Her expression is glum, her lips are pursed.

"Is something wrong?"

That would be an understatement. She moved over two weeks ago now, and Fadila cannot understand why her son has not come to see her even once: he lives a hundred yards away from the hostel. The day before yesterday, Sunday evening, after she had waited all weekend for at least a phone call, she couldn't stand it any longer. She called him.

Her son told her straight up that he didn't like the fact she'd moved to Pantin because his wife didn't like it.

"It's typical," says Édith. "She's afraid you'll be over at their place all the time."

Of course, wails Fadila. But it's this very hypothesis that makes her so angry. She's never tried to impose at her son's house, she's never found fault with her daughter-in-law about anything, she's never criticized in any way, even implicitly. "I never saying I need this, I need that, the way other old women is doing, I never asking for money."

"I thought your daughter-in-law liked you?"

Fadila doesn't think so: "She no say nothing but she never looking in the eye. After she go talking my son."

She sits with her hands between her knees. There are days when the work can just wait a while. It wasn't her idea, after all, to move into this hostel in Pantin. She didn't even know it existed. She wasn't the one who went to find out whether she could get in and how to apply.

After her son first mentioned it, she went over to his place to discuss it, on purpose, in her daughter-in-law's presence. The young woman did not seem to be particularly reticent. Later, just after she found out she'd been given a spot at the hostel, she had lunch with them; it was two days later, a Sunday, she remembers. She spoke openly of how pleased she was, turning to her little two-year-old granddaughter and saying, right in front of her daughter-in-law: "I say I taking the little girls to the park on Wednesdays with sandwiches." Now she seems to recall that her daughter-in-law fell silent at that point. "She thinking I going her place before I going to the park. Is not true! I take the little girls and I go, I don't see her!"

Édith reasons with her. It will work out. In a little while, once Fadila has shown them she knows how to be discreet, and that she will never show up at their door uninvited, her daughter-in-law will be reassured. She'll come around.

Fadila shakes her head wordlessly.

"You'll see," insists Édith, "your son will be in touch very soon. He's a good son, you've always said as much. He's kind."

"He's kind but is changing."

She wipes her eye.

"Is daughter-in-law never like mother-in-law."

"It's because they're rivals. They love the same man. And in general the husbands show that they prefer their wife."

Fadila nods her head. She knows this as well as Édith.

"Yesterday I crying," she says. "All my life I crying."

She is getting ready to leave, her long coat buttoned up to her neck and her black headscarf pulled tight around her head, when the door opens. It is Gilles, home earlier than usual. He has a big bouquet of flowers in his hand, little roses of a ravishing color, which he bought for no particular reason as he was walking by the florist's, something he does from time to time.

"Here," he says to Fadila. He pulls the bouquet apart and holds out half of it to her.

She stands there with her arms tight against her body.

"Nobody is never giving me flowers, not me."

"Well, all the more reason, then," says Gilles.

As she watches her, Édith wonders whether Fadila is not about to succumb to her emotion. Perhaps that is what Fadila herself is afraid of, as she tucks the flowers between her elbow and her side and says simply, "Thank you, then. Goodbye."

Little Paul has constant chalazions and his eyelids are swollen. Fadila knows what it is.

"Has to use orange flower water, is making germs go away."

"Have you seen all the medication he has?"

"Is medication no doing no good. Is orange flower water is good for everything. You putting on cotton when he go to bed, you washing his eyes. Even for the heart is very good."

She is in better spirits. Her son and daughter-in-law came to see her on Sunday, with her granddaughters. They all went for a walk, the weather was fine.

Fadila herself volunteers this information, while she's having a little coffee break in the kitchen.

Yesterday she went to the police *préfecture* to renew her residence permit. She waited in line for hours. And once it was her turn, since she had just moved, things got complicated. She didn't leave with a new permit. They are supposed to send it to her.

"There's no problem, then?" asks Édith. "You'll get your permit?"

"Me, I never had no problems with permit," says Fadila confidently. "I been careful. I no have the courage do stupid things."

34

S he pulls up a chair next to Édith and sits down heavily. "Has to begin again," she says.

"With pleasure," says Édith approvingly, trying to make her tone as light as if they had never interrupted their lessons.

But she remembers how Fadila had asked to go "slow-slow" after an earlier interruption, and that even then they were starting over.

"Would you like to work on the numbers for a while?"

That is fine with Fadila, particularly as she has a new telephone number. She's making do without a landline: Aïcha has given her a cell phone.

"That's very kind of her," remarks Édith.

"No, is no kind, she having another, is give me old one. Is no kind, Aïcha."

"She helped you move."

"Yes, and after she no phoning, never! Is one month, maybe more. She be selfish-center."

SELFISH, writes Édith at the top of a blank sheet, pronouncing the word at the same time. And below it: *06*.

"You know all the cell phone numbers begin with *06*. Which is lucky for you, because those are two numbers you write easily."

She has the impression she is pulling on an extremely fragile string. But Fadila copies the two numbers perfectly.

They go back over the eight other ones. "By the way," says

Édith, "you will have to give me your new address. We'll learn to write it, too."

"Is next time I bringing," says Fadila.

She copies out her new telephone number once, then gets up: "Give me paper, I studying at home."

Édith called Fadila that morning to tell her that this afternoon she won't be alone. She'll be working at home with an English novelist, a close acquaintance. Her French is good and she wants to go over the translations of her books carefully. Édith has no objections; on the contrary.

Fadila keeps out of the way that afternoon. When she is ready to leave, Édith and Magdalena Wright are still at work. She sticks her head through the door and with a smile she says, "Well then, goodbye, girls!"

She wants to learn new words. Just as well, thinks Édith. No point in dwelling on what she has most probably forgotten.

"What are your granddaughters' names?" she asks. "Your son's two girls."

Nabila and Zaina. "All letters you know," says Édith, writing the two names in big letters.

She takes the opportunity to inquire about them. Fadila is delighted that the older girl, not yet three, is always asking to write. Her mother gives her paper and pencils and the little girl covers the paper with big circles.

"Is like that when you speaking a lot to the children they little," says Fadila. She finds her daughter-in-law somewhat evasive, and she thinks she should stop breast-feeding the younger girl, who's ten months old, and go and look for work. Still, she cannot help but admire the educated woman in her, and she knows that, undeniably, she is a good mother.

Fadila opens the main door downstairs and comes upon

Édith in the entrance with a mop and a bucket. There was a broken bottle, wine has spilled on the tiles. The building has no concierge, and the cleaning of the shared space is done only once a week by a cleaning company.

"Is you cleaning this?" scolds Fadila. "Why is no that lady she looking after the garbage cans?"

The woman in question, a young North African whom Fadila has already run into, takes the containers in and out, nothing more, explains Édith, she doesn't do any cleaning.

Fadila interrupts her: "She has head in the air. Is Algerian."

And in answer to Édith's questioning look: "Is proud. Is Algerians they has head in the air. Is saying they French, no want to do cleaning."

Édith writes *ZAINA* just below *AÏCHA*, and tries to make Fadila see what the two words have in common. Fadila sees the *A*'s, but not the *I*'s with their little dieresis on top.

Nor does she recognize the word *AÏCHA* anymore.

Then Édith writes *ZAINA* and under that, *ZORA*.

"And these two names, Zaina and Zora (she stresses the *Z*), what do they have that's the same?"

Fadila points to the *A* in *Zora*.

"You know the *A* really well," Édith congratulates her.

She has brought back out the "treasure chest" of the words Fadila acquired so slowly the previous year. She copies it out for her—it takes her all of a minute—hands it to her, and says, "These are the words we spent a lot of time on, you know them. You can copy them out at home, we'll go back over them next week."

But Édith needs something to take her to the next stage. At the rate they're working, one step forward, two steps back, they will lose heart. Fadila will soon be so discouraged she won't want to go on.

Édith calls her cousin Sara. She knows what she's looking for, now. Fadila needs a private teacher, a real one, someone like a retired professor, who will give her at least three classes a week.

Sara is not too optimistic. But she has some friends who know more than she does about the milieu of literacy learning, and she's willing to give them a ring.

She calls back two days later. Édith will be pleased: the parish of Saint-Séverin, in Paris, have founded an association that offers personalized literacy classes.

"Private lessons?" asks Édith, who can scarcely believe her ears.

"Precisely. The teachers meet with students one on one. It's made to measure."

Édith calls the person in charge. Her cousin was right. They have to find a time slot but almost all the teachers are retirees, volunteers, and in general have a fair amount of free time. Also, Fadila must be willing to go to the premises of the association for her classes, opposite the church of Saint-Séverin—although there are a few volunteers who are willing to go elsewhere for the lesson, or who don't mind working from home.

There are all sorts of possibilities. All Fadila has to do is go by the association one day and sign up, they'll talk it over.

35

W hat's the matter?" asks Édith, who knows now that
she has cause to be worried when Fadila walks in
without saying a word, not even hello.

"Is crying, crying."

It turns out that Nasser and his family have moved away
from Pantin. It took all of three days. They'd been wanting to
move for months. They had put their name down here and
there. In the end Auchan, Nasser's employer, found him a
place to live, a good-sized apartment, near his work.

Nasser and his wife couldn't stand their two hundred
square feet anymore. They immediately said yes and on
Saturday they moved. They're absolutely thrilled: they now
have a real two-bedroom in a new building.

"Is it far from Pantin?"

"Is very far, way other side," she said, with a wave, "at the
end the RER A, at Maison de la Fête."

Édith unfolds a map of the RER.

"You mean Maisons-Laffitte?"

"Yes, is Maison de la Fête."

"Put yourself in their shoes: how could they say no? At last
they have a proper place to live. Some day soon you can look
for a place nearby. Your son will help you find something."

No, she says. She just had her residence permit renewed, with
her new address in Pantin. She can't keep moving all the time.

And anyway, she wants to go back to Morocco. She's been
thinking about it more and more. "Is my brother he wants I

coming. Is big house. Is people stay in France they no go nowhere."

Look at her neighbors at the hostel. "They going market is the morning, is coming home, is watching television. They say they is staying because the health care. But is health care no stop you dying! Is in Morocco everything you need. If you getting sick, is hospital."

Work on her letters? Today? She puts on a sorry face: "You thinking I manage learning with everything is happen now?"

Édith will wait for a more auspicious moment to tell her about the classes in Saint-Séverin.

Two days ago, April 22nd, the first round of the presidential elections was held. As was to be expected, the remaining candidates are Ségolène Royal and Nicolas Sarkozy.

All the papers imply that the immigrants are dreading a Sarkozy victory.

"You know," says Édith, "if Nicolas Sarkozy wins, it won't be what we call a disaster. It won't change much for you."

Fadila reacts sharply: "'Course is no disaster! Is people saying Sarkozy is disaster, but I no saying. You know what is problem? Is Sarkozy he say the truth. What is French people they say? Truth hurts?"

"I go seeing Nasser there Maison de la Fête: is like Côte d'Azur! Is nice place! Is no Blacks, no Arabs. They got two bedrooms, one bedroom for daughter, one bedroom for parents. Is baby in the buggy very happy, they open window is trees. They on the ground floor and just outside is garden.

"Is very good place. Little girls going to has good upbringing, is nobody but French people there. Is no like in Pantin is children saying bad words in the street. Is nothing like that there.

"Little granddaughter her father he scare her, he say, 'Is all over, we moving back to Pantin, let's go,' he pretending to take suitcase. She cry and cry. She no want."

"Listen, I've heard about a new course that would be great for you: with a teacher just for you. You know, what they call private lessons."

"Don't go bother this thing now," she says. "I going back to Morocco soon."

"It will take you a while to prepare your departure. The paperwork for retirement takes a long time. In the meanwhile you'll be able to take a few classes. You'll go much faster with a real teacher. It's free. You can start whenever you want, not only in September."

"We'll see," she says.

But her tone has changed.

"You right, I gotta. Is good thing I no forgetting is write my name."

Nicolas Sarkozy has been elected President of the Republic. "I very happy," says Fadila. "Everyone around me they very happy. Is people they doing trafficking they no happy. Sarkozy say he gonna clean up, is right. Is what he gotta do."

On May 10th, at eight o'clock in the morning, Fadila is hit by a car, not far from her place in Pantin. Her children don't know what she was doing out so early: perhaps she wanted to use a public telephone to save on her cell phone minutes. All she had on her were her keys and her wallet. The driver who hit her says she didn't see her. It was raining.

There were witnesses. Fadila cried out and fell to the ground and lost consciousness. At the hospital where she has been taken they have diagnosed a brain trauma, along with a fractured pelvis and superficial injuries. She is in a coma, with artificial respiration.

36

Eleven days after the accident the doctor summons Fadila's children to the hospital. The cerebral hematoma has resorbed somewhat, and they were able to perform a brain scan. The prognosis is not good. There are multiple cerebral lesions. If Fadila comes out of the coma, she will be severely handicapped. She will not be able to see, or hear, or speak.

"Poor thing," says her daughter Aïcha, "and here she was about to take her retirement any day now. Bad enough that she never had any luck in life: she never even got to have any rest. She was talking about going back to Morocco. She thought she might try to spend six months there and six months here.

"I was urging her to retire, but she wanted to go on working to continue helping her son."

She is in reanimation, in a room where, apparently, the door is always left wide open.

Édith hesitates in the doorway. She does not recognize Fadila. The woman lying there in the reclining bed, in line with the door, has several tubes in her mouth and nostrils, and it is hard to see her face. Her arms are bared, like her shoulders, and are attached along the side of her body, over a tightly pulled sheet. Her hair on the pillow is uncombed, fanned out on either side of her head.

On seeing those round shoulders and arms, her smooth

golden skin, her long curly black hair, Édith thinks she is in the presence of a much younger woman. She must have gotten the wrong room.

She walks in and reads the papers posted on the wall. On one of them she finds what she was looking for: *AMRANI FADILA* and, underneath, *severe brain trauma*.

After three weeks Fadila emerges from the coma. From time to time she moves, or opens her eyes. But she has not regained consciousness for all that. She still requires artificial respiration, she cannot do without.

Édith is in the room when a woman comes in and introduces herself: she is the neurologist. The woman is categorical: they must not have any false hopes. The patient is in a vegetative state. She cannot swallow, she has no feeding reflexes and will need a feeding tube. When they ask her to make a gesture, she does not react. She cannot see anymore. She cannot hear.

"And then there is everything we can see on the scan. Irreversible lesions. But we can't know everything," says the doctor on leaving. "To what degree is she conscious? That's the big question. Talk to her, above all. Touch her, take her hand."

The room has fallen silent, save for the quiet purr of a machine and a few irregular clicking sounds. Fadila's eyes are closed, and she is as motionless as a recumbent statue; Édith cannot even see her breathing under the sheet. Without making a sound Édith sits down beside her, on her right, and places her hand on Fadila's. She cannot bring herself to talk to her out loud. The warmth of her skin reminds her of the rare times when she held that hand in hers, to write with her.

A cruel thought comes to her. If they were to try to communicate with Fadila by showing her one letter after the other, so that she could express herself by blinking her eyelids—one blink for *A*, two blinks for *B*, and so on, like the character in

The Count of Monte Cristo or, more recently, two or three individuals who sustained severe head injuries yet managed to dictate entire books in this way—well, it would be impossible. In her palm Édith feels, achingly, the throb of the alpha and omega of her failure. She did not know how to teach Fadila the alphabet. She was not able to make her understand how to use writing to combine letters in order to make words that are legible; surely that would have given Fadila access to the language of the locked-in, a language that is neither oral nor written, a language born of the worst imaginable solitude, and the only way out of it.

EUROPA EDITIONS BACKLIST
(alphabetical by author)

Fiction

Carmine Abate
Between Two Seas • 978-1-933372-40-2 • Territories: World
The Homecoming Party • 978-1-933372-83-9 • Territories: World

Milena Agus
From the Land of the Moon • 978-1-60945-001-4 • Ebook • Territories:
World (excl. ANZ)

Salwa Al Neimi
The Proof of the Honey • 978-1-933372-68-6 • Ebook • Territories: World
(excl UK)

Simonetta Agnello Hornby
The Nun • 978-1-60945-062-5 • Territories: World

Daniel Arsand
Lovers • 978-1-60945-071-7 • Ebook • Territories: World

Jenn Ashworth
A Kind of Intimacy • 978-1-933372-86-0 • Territories: US & Can

Beryl Bainbridge
The Girl in the Polka Dot Dress • 978-1-60945-056-4 • Ebook •
Territories: US

Muriel Barbery
The Elegance of the Hedgehog • 978-1-933372-60-0 • Ebook • Territories:
World (excl. UK & EU)
Gourmet Rhapsody • 978-1-933372-95-2 • Ebook • Territories: World
(excl. UK & EU)

Stefano Benni
Margherita Dolce Vita • 978-1-933372-20-4 • Territories: World
Timeskipper • 978-1-933372-44-0 • Territories: World

Romano Bilenchi
The Chill • 978-1-933372-90-7 • Territories: World

Kazimierz Brandys
Rondo • 978-1-60945-004-5 • Territories: World

Alina Bronsky
Broken Glass Park • 978-1-933372-96-9 • Ebook • Territories: World
The Hottest Dishes of the Tartar Cuisine • 978-1-60945-006-9 • Ebook •
Territories: World

Jesse Browner
Everything Happens Today • 978-1-60945-051-9 • Ebook • Territories:
World (excl. UK & EU)

Francisco Coloane
Tierra del Fuego • 978-1-933372-63-1 • Ebook • Territories: World

Rebecca Connell
The Art of Losing • 978-1-933372-78-5 • Territories: US

Laurence Cossé
A Novel Bookstore • 978-1-933372-82-2 • Ebook • Territories: World
An Accident in August • 978-1-60945-049-6 • Territories: World (excl. UK)

Diego De Silva
I Hadn't Understood • 978-1-60945-065-6 • Territories: World

Shashi Deshpande
The Dark Holds No Terrors • 978-1-933372-67-9 • Territories: US

Steve Erickson
Zeroville • 978-1-933372-39-6 • Territories: US & Can
These Dreams of You • 978-1-60945-063-2 • Territories: US & Can

Elena Ferrante
The Days of Abandonment • 978-1-933372-00-6 • Ebook • Territories: World
Troubling Love • 978-1-933372-16-7 • Territories: World
The Lost Daughter • 978-1-933372-42-6 • Territories: World

Linda Ferri
Cecilia • 978-1-933372-87-7 • Territories: World

Damon Galgut
In a Strange Room • 978-1-60945-011-3 • Ebook • Territories: USA

Santiago Gamboa
Necropolis • 978-1-60945-073-1 • Ebook • Territories: World

Jane Gardam
Old Filth • 978-1-933372-13-6 • Ebook • Territories: US
The Queen of the Tambourine • 978-1-933372-36-5 • Ebook • Territories: US
The People on Privilege Hill • 978-1-933372-56-3 • Ebook • Territories: US
The Man in the Wooden Hat • 978-1-933372-89-1 • Ebook • Territories: US
God on the Rocks • 978-1-933372-76-1 • Ebook • Territories: US
Crusoe's Daughter • 978-1-60945-069-4 • Ebook • Territories: US

Anna Gavalda
French Leave • 978-1-60945-005-2 • Ebook • Territories: US & Can

Seth Greenland
The Angry Buddhist • 978-1-60945-068-7 • Ebook • Territories: World

Katharina Hacker
The Have-Nots • 978-1-933372-41-9 • Territories: World (excl. India)

Patrick Hamilton
Hangover Square • 978-1-933372-06-8 • Territories: US & Can

James Hamilton-Paterson
Cooking with Fernet Branca • 978-1-933372-01-3 • Territories: US
Amazing Disgrace • 978-1-933372-19-8 • Territories: US
Rancid Pansies • 978-1-933372-62-4 • Territories: USA

Alfred Hayes
The Girl on the Via Flaminia • 978-1-933372-24-2 • Ebook •
Territories: World

Jean-Claude Izzo
The Lost Sailors • 978-1-933372-35-8 • Territories: World
A Sun for the Dying • 978-1-933372-59-4 • Territories: World

Gail Jones
Sorry • 978-1-933372-55-6 • Territories: US & Can

Ioanna Karystiani
The Jasmine Isle • 978-1-933372-10-5 • Territories: World
Swell • 978-1-933372-98-3 • Territories: World

Peter Kocan
Fresh Fields • 978-1-933372-29-7 • Territories: US, EU & Can
The Treatment and the Cure • 978-1-933372-45-7 • Territories: US, EU & Can

Helmut Krausser
Eros • 978-1-933372-58-7 • Territories: World

Amara Lakhous
Clash of Civilizations Over an Elevator in Piazza Vittorio •
978-1-933372-61-7 • Ebook • Territories: World
Divorce Islamic Style • 978-1-60945-066-3 • Ebook • Territories: World

Lia Levi
The Jewish Husband • 978-1-933372-93-8 • Territories: World

Valerio Massimo Manfredi
The Ides of March • 978-1-933372-99-0 • Territories: US

Leïla Marouane
The Sexual Life of an Islamist in Paris • 978-1-933372-85-3 •
Territories: World

Lorenzo Mediano
The Frost on His Shoulders • 978-1-60945-072-4 • Ebook •
Territories: World

Sélim Nassib
I Loved You for Your Voice • 978-1-933372-07-5 • Territories: World
The Palestinian Lover • 978-1-933372-23-5 • Territories: World

Amélie Nothomb
Tokyo Fiancée • 978-1-933372-64-8 • Territories: US & Can
Hygiene and the Assassin • 978-1-933372-77-8 • Ebook • Territories: US & Can

Valeria Parrella
For Grace Received • 978-1-933372-94-5 • Territories: World

Alessandro Piperno
The Worst Intentions • 978-1-933372-33-4 • Territories: World
Persecution • 978-1-60945-074-8 • Ebook • Territories: World

Lorcan Roche
The Companion • 978-1-933372-84-6 • Territories: World

Boualem Sansal
The German Mujahid • 978-1-933372-92-1 • Ebook • Territories: US & Can

Eric-Emmanuel Schmitt
The Most Beautiful Book in the World • 978-1-933372-74-7 • Ebook •
Territories: World
The Woman with the Bouquet • 978-1-933372-81-5 • Ebook • Territories:
US & Can

Angelika Schrobsdorff
You Are Not Like Other Mothers • 978-1-60945-075-5 • Ebook •
Territories: World

Audrey Schulman
Three Weeks in December • 978-1-60945-064-9 • Ebook • Territories: US
& Can

James Scudamore
Heliopolis • 978-1-933372-73-0 • Ebook • Territories: US

Luis Sepúlveda
The Shadow of What We Were • 978-1-60945-002-1 • Ebook • Territories:
World

Paolo Sorrentino
Everybody's Right • 978-1-60945-052-6 • Ebook • Territories: US & Can

Domenico Starnone
First Execution • 978-1-933372-66-2 • Territories: World

Henry Sutton
Get Me out of Here • 978-1-60945-007-6 • Ebook • Territories: US & Can

Chad Taylor
Departure Lounge • 978-1-933372-09-9 • Territories: US, EU & Can

Roma Tearne
Mosquito • 978-1-933372-57-0 • Territories: US & Can
Bone China • 978-1-933372-75-4 • Territories: US

André Carl van der Merwe
Moffie • 978-1-60945-050-2 • Ebook • Territories: World
(excl. S. Africa)

Fay Weldon
Chalcot Crescent • 978-1-933372-79-2 • Territories: US

Anne Wiazemsky
My Berlin Child • 978-1-60945-003-8 • Territories: US & Can

Jonathan Yardley
Second Reading • 978-1-60945-008-3 • Ebook • Territories: US & Can

Edwin M. Yoder Jr.
Lions at Lamb House • 978-1-933372-34-1 • Territories: World

Michele Zackheim
Broken Colors • 978-1-933372-37-2 • Territories: World

Alice Zeniter
Take This Man • 978-1-60945-053-3 • Territories: World

Tonga Books

Ian Holding
Of Beasts and Beings • 978-1-60945-054-0 • Ebook • Territories: US & Can

Sara Levine
Treasure Island!!! • 978-0-14043-768-3 • Ebook • Territories: World

Alexander Maksik
You Deserve Nothing • 978-1-60945-048-9 • Ebook • Territories: US, Can & EU (excl. UK)

Thad Ziolkowski
Wichita • 978-1-60945-070-0 • Ebook • Territories: World

Crime/Noir

Massimo Carlotto
The Goodbye Kiss • 978-1-933372-05-1 • Ebook • Territories: World
Death's Dark Abyss • 978-1-933372-18-1 • Ebook • Territories: World
The Fugitive • 978-1-933372-25-9 • Ebook • Territories: World
Bandit Love • 978-1-933372-80-8 • Ebook • Territories: World
Poisonville • 978-1-933372-91-4 • Ebook • Territories: World

Giancarlo De Cataldo
The Father and the Foreigner • 978-1-933372-72-3 • Territories: World

Caryl Férey
Zulu • 978-1-933372-88-4 • Ebook • Territories: World (excl. UK & EU)
Utu • 978-1-60945-055-7 • Ebook • Territories: World (excl. UK & EU)

Alicia Giménez-Bartlett
Dog Day • 978-1-933372-14-3 • Territories: US & Can
Prime Time Suspect • 978-1-933372-31-0 • Territories: US & Can
Death Rites • 978-1-933372-54-9 • Territories: US & Can

Jean-Claude Izzo
Total Chaos • 978-1-933372-04-4 • Territories: US & Can
Chourmo • 978-1-933372-17-4 • Territories: US & Can
Solea • 978-1-933372-30-3 • Territories: US & Can

Matthew F. Jones
Boot Tracks • 978-1-933372-11-2 • Territories: US & Can

Gene Kerrigan
The Midnight Choir • 978-1-933372-26-6 • Territories: US & Can
Little Criminals • 978-1-933372-43-3 • Territories: US & Can

Carlo Lucarelli
Carte Blanche • 978-1-933372-15-0 • Territories: World
The Damned Season • 978-1-933372-27-3 • Territories: World
Via delle Oche • 978-1-933372-53-2 • Territories: World

Edna Mazya
Love Burns • 978-1-933372-08-2 • Territories: World (excl. ANZ)

Yishai Sarid
Limassol • 978-1-60945-000-7 • Ebook • Territories: World (excl. UK, AUS & India)

Joel Stone
The Jerusalem File • 978-1-933372-65-5 • Ebook • Territories: World

Benjamin Tammuz
Minotaur • 978-1-933372-02-0 • Ebook • Territories: World

Non-fiction

Alberto Angela
A Day in the Life of Ancient Rome • 978-1-933372-71-6 • Territories: World • History

Helmut Dubiel
Deep In the Brain: Living with Parkinson's Disease • 978-1-933372-70-9 •
Ebook • Territories: World • Medicine/Memoir

James Hamilton-Paterson
Seven-Tenths: The Sea and Its Thresholds • 978-1-933372-69-3 • Territories:
USA • Nature/Essays

Daniele Mastrogiacomo
Days of Fear • 978-1-933372-97-6 • Ebook • Territories: World • Current
affairs/Memoir/Afghanistan/Journalism

Valery Panyushkin
Twelve Who Don't Agree • 978-1-60945-010-6 • Ebook • Territories:
World • Current affairs/Memoir/Russia/Journalism

Christa Wolf
One Day a Year: 1960-2000 • 978-1-933372-22-8 • Territories: World •
Memoir/History/20th Century

Children's Illustrated Fiction

Altan
Here Comes Timpa • 978-1-933372-28-0 • Territories: World (excl. Italy)
Timpa Goes to the Sea • 978-1-933372-32-7 • Territories: World (excl. Italy)
Fairy Tale Timpa • 978-1-933372-38-9 • Territories: World (excl. Italy)

Wolf Erlbruch
The Big Question • 978-1-933372-03-7 • Territories: US & Can
The Miracle of the Bears • 978-1-933372-21-1 • Territories: US & Can
(with **Gioconda Belli**) *The Butterfly Workshop* • 978-1-933372-12-9 •
Territories: US & Can